THE
DEDD HOUSE

JAMEY LEVIER

BALBOA.
PRESS

A DIVISION OF HAY HOUSE

Balboa Press books may be ordered through booksellers or by contacting:

Balboa Press
A Division of Hay House
1663 Liberty Drive
Bloomington, IN 47403
www.balboapress.com
1 (877) 407-4847

Print information available on the last page.

ISBN: 978-1-5043-7196-4 (sc)
ISBN: 978-1-5043-7197-1 (hc)
ISBN: 978-1-5043-7218-3 (e)

Library of Congress Control Number: 2016921018

Balboa Press rev. date: 01/09/2017

DEDICATION

This book is dedicated to my best friend, most trusted confidant and wife, Jennifer LeVier, without whom this book would not exist. Her long-suffering patience with me through hundreds of hours of writing, editing and re-writing while I was locked away in my office is a faithful testament to our committed journey together.

Thank you Jennifer for loving me, believing in me, and going with me on this adventure called life. You make my dreams come true, because you believe in them too.

ACKNOWLEDGMENTS

Jennifer LeVier – My wife, co-editor, and to a great extent *Jennifer* in the book. Her support was invaluable.

Nancy Cunningham – My neighbor in Valdosta, Ga and retired English teacher, willing to take an honest red pen to the text.

Robert Gernale – Cover artist. (rgernale@yahoo.com)

Dr. Wayne Dyer – My spiritual advisor; he taught me to think from the end, imagining the book is already a NY Times best seller, to be there in that moment at all times, and to assume the feeling of my wish fulfilled.

Bill Stainton – A 29-time Emmy Award winning TV producer. I met Bill in Savannah, GA in 2015 while attending his creativity workshop. Many of Bill's Ezine articles motivated me to push through to the end of this long journey. When you commit to something, people are sent into your life at the right time to help you get to the finish line. Bill was one of those people for me.

Finally, I wish to acknowledge artistic inspiration received from my cousin, Keith Allen, lead singer and song writer for the band *Bleeding In Stereo*. I was so proud to be a special guest when Keith opened for *3 Doors Down* in 2015. Rock on, you creative genius.

INTRODUCTION

And it called itself The Dedd House....

It was a chilly October night, 2013, in Hernando, Mississippi, just south of Memphis, TN. I awoke from a vivid dream at 3:00 AM, one that left me feeling like it really happened. I had these types of dreams before, but this one was different.

I spent the next few days in its residue. It wouldn't leave me alone, like a pesky fly. I brushed it aside several times, and back it would come with stronger intent. So I gave into it.

I scripted everything I could remember, and several hours later I was holding five pages of an outline. It looked like it had potential for a book, but there was no ending.

I let the outline simmer for a couple weeks in my office. Still, it wouldn't leave me alone. It was screaming, "Write me! Write me!"

No, I thought, *there's no ending*! "Don't worry about the ending," it said, "I've got your back."

So I started to write. Thirty days later there were one hundred eighty pages…and still no ending. November 30th rolled around. No ending. *Where is this going?* I thought.

And then, another vivid dream. I woke up (again at 3:00 AM) yelling, "Yes! That's it!"

My wife was startled awake. "What's wrong honey?" she asked.

"I know how it's going to end!"

"That's awesome, baby," she replied. "You better write it down."

I rushed to my writing chair and penned the ending as quickly as my hand would go, and then returned to bed in awe of what just happened.

Three years later, here it is, a complete story: The Dedd House… my child – nurtured and ready to be sent out into the world.

Sometimes the Universe throws things at us we don't expect, or even understand, and it relies on us to trust it. It then nudges us over and over to take action. Without that continual nudge, this book you are holding in your hands (or reading on your tablet) would not exist.

So, to the Universe I am grateful, and I say thank you for not allowing me to brush this aside. It's supposed to be here.

WARNING: Strong language, violence and explicit sexual content. Nobody under 18 should read this.

To Jennifer:

Your beauty drips onto my heart
Like sweet morning dew
Giving the sun its shine
And my soul its muse

Your passion caresses my spirit
Like a gently flowing stream
Giving voice to my silence
And my heart its dream

Thoughts of you flood my day
Like a mid-day meadow swarm
Giving joy to my sadness
And peace to my storm

I love you forever, and then some…

-Danny

CHAPTER 1

An obese man sat next to me on the plane. He said they made him buy two tickets, and it was unfair. The arm rest beside me had to remain up because it was digging into his side. He had to use a seat belt extension.

He was excited to be going to Memphis for the first time, to see Graceland and Beale Street.

"You from there?" he asked.

His halitosis was overpowering, and he must not have showered for a few days. I looked out the window. "Yes, I grew up near there."

"Where?"

"Tunica, Mississippi."

He was still adjusting himself to get comfy, bumping into me. "Oh, I want to go there too. I hear the casinos pay great."

I took shallow breaths through my mouth. "Yep."

I opened the air nozzle and pointed it toward him, hoping to clear the stench. No luck.

Thank God we departed on time.

CHAPTER 2

I tried to sleep, but he wouldn't shut up.

They served pretzels and Coke. His tray table was jammed against his belly. I gave him my pretzels, hoping to get a reprieve from his incessant chattering.

He chewed with his mouth open, and kept talking. A speck of chewed pretzel shot from his mouth and landed in my full cup of Coke. I was certain he saw it, but he just kept gobbling those pretzels, slurping the Coke and talking.

"That's a cool tattoo on your forearm," he said, tapping it with his index finger. I unwittingly jerked away, but he didn't seem to mind.

He reminded me of the chubby kid from the movie *Bad Santa*, all grown up, still fixing sandwiches.

"You in the Navy?" he asked.

"Mmm-hmm," I nodded.

"You a Captain or something? My uncle was a Captain. Although you look too young to be a Captain. You look like you're in good shape though. Almost in good a shape as me!" His booming laugh filled the cabin.

I didn't want to encourage him, but I couldn't hold back a chuckle.

"That fat guy stinks!" shouted a little boy in front of us.

"Shush. Don't be rude," said the lady beside him.

I felt embarrassed for my seat mate.

He finished the pretzels and asked if I was going to drink my Coke.

"No, you can have it," I said.

"Tell me friend, what do you do in the Navy?"

I pulled my T-shirt collar over my nose to avoid the halitosis, pretending to wipe off something. "I'm a fighter pilot."

"No way! Thanks for your service, man!"

"No problem."

He chugged my Coke, giving me a chance to catch my breath. But not for long.

"How long you been in the Navy?"

I did the T-shirt thing again. "I just got out of flight school in Pensacola."

"You got an assignment yet?"

"Yes, but if I told you, I'd have to kill you."

His laugh filled the cabin again. A white drop of his spittle landed on my arm.

"Sorry about that," he said.

I wiped it off with a tiny napkin. "No worries."

The flight attendant collected our garbage.

She looked at me. "Would you like something else, sir?" She must have seen him take mine.

I smiled. "No thanks. I'm full."

She winked at me and walked on.

He tapped my leg. "I bet you get a lot of chicks."

"I'm married."

He elbowed my ribs, snickering. "Yeah, but that doesn't plug any holes, right?"

I heard a female behind us mumble, "Oh my God."

T-shirt maneuver. "My wife is my soulmate."

"Nice. What's her name?"

"Jennifer."

"Where'd you meet?"

"Ole Miss."

"Go Rebels!"

"Mmm-hmm."

"You got any kids?"

"One on the way. A little boy."

"Very nice. Pick out any names yet?"

I looked out the window. "No names yet." I lied.

"What's your name?"

"Danny."

"Danny what?"

"Danny Dedd."

His questioning was so rapid I felt like I was in an episode of *Dragnet*, which my dad made me watch with him in my pre-teen years. Joe Friday had nothing on this guy.

"That's a cool last name. Like, as in 'you're dead'?" He made a cutthroat sign.

"No, spelled D-E-D-D."

"I bet you have a cool call sign, like 'Killer' or 'Grave Digger.'"

"No, it's Zombie."

"Awesome. By the way, I'm Chuck. Chuck Timblin."

He wanted to shake my hand, but I had just seen him pick his nose. I held up my fist instead. "I'm a fist bumper, Chuck. No offense."

"Blow it up, Danny!"

I was reluctant, but I did it anyway.

I told him I was going to take a nap.

"Sure thing. Don't let me keep you up, soldier."

I dreamt about Jennifer. We were in The Grove at Ole Miss, making out.

I woke up an hour later and realized I had a boner. I adjusted and rubbed my eyes.

"Hey, Danny, is that the Mississippi River down there?"

"Yep."

He leaned across me to get a closer look. His ear was full of wax and there were white specks in his greasy hair. I fought off a gag reflex.

"I can't wait to see Graceland. You ever been there?"

"Yep."

"What's that?" he said, pointing.

"I can't see anything."

"Right there. Hey, that's downtown, right? What's that big shiny pyramid-looking thing?"

"You'll have to lean back for me to see out the window."

"Sorry, man. Right down there. What's that?"

"That's the Pyramid."

He tapped my leg again. "You're joking, right?"

"Nope."

"I'd like to see that too. What's in it?"

T-shirt maneuver. "Nothing."

"Really? Nothing?"

"Nothing."

I was happy when a man behind us spoke up. "The Grizzlies used to play there, and then they built the FedEx Forum. It's been empty for a long time. Rumor has it, Bass Pro Shops might buy it."

Chuck turned his head as far as he could, "Thank you, sir. You from Memphis?"

"My whole life," said the man.

The pilot made an announcement to prepare the cabin for landing. *Thank you, Jesus.*

CHAPTER 3

I turned on my cell phone before the plane came to a complete stop. It could not power up fast enough. All I wanted to hear was the sweet sound of Jennifer's voice. It went to voicemail. *Shit.* I left a message. "Hey, baby, we just landed. Can't wait to see you. Remember, Delta flight 703 from Jacksonville. Love you."

I called my dad's cell phone. Voicemail.

Mom's cell phone. Voicemail.

Chuck struggled to get out of his seat. I gave him a helping nudge. I didn't want to touch him, but at this point I would have eaten a cat turd covered in litter sprinkles to get off this plane faster.

Chuck ungracefully maneuvered himself into the aisle and opened the overhead bin. The plane was already empty in front of him. People behind us were growing restless. He must have sensed it. "Sorry, folks. It's not easy being 500 pounds."

I wasn't sure why, but my eyes welled up a bit. Despite Chuck's annoyance, I suddenly felt an affinity for him.

I followed him down the aisle, wondering what it felt like to be him, having to make special accommodations wherever he went.

Nonetheless, I was anxious to see my loved ones. I darted around him first chance in the jetway, along with several other impatient passengers.

He yelled as I ran past, "Nice talking to you, Danny! Congrats on your little boy!"

I waved blindly and yelled, "Thank you, Chuck!"

CHAPTER 4

Memphis International Airport was not crowded. I was able to jog freely to baggage claim with my duffle bag. I called Jennifer and my parents again. All voicemail.

Give me a break!

I stood at the baggage turnstile forever. The buzzer finally sounded and bags started rolling out. Several people from the flight were complaining. I looked around. No Chuck. I wondered how he was managing.

I texted Jennifer. "I'm here! Where are u guys?"

Thankfully both of my suitcases came out together. I rolled them through the exit, hoping to see my dad's car waiting outside.

I stepped into an oven. The dense, hot air packed an unforgiving punch against my body. I had forgotten about the noxious mix of heat and humidity in Memphis. Pensacola was hot, but not like this.

I watched several cars come and go, picking up passengers. I called again. All voicemail. No texts.

My hair was soaked. Sweat was burning my eyes. I felt a droplet roll down my spine and into the crack of my ass. I shuffled and twitched to relieve the itch. Normally, I'd just reach around and take care of it. But not in public. I couldn't wait to ask Jennifer if she'd like some ass gravy. I laughed out loud. It was a momentary reprieve from my anxiousness.

Where are they?

My phone alerted me of an incoming text.

It's about time!

It was my buddy, asking if I made it home okay. I didn't respond.

I called the house phone. No answer.

I debated taking a taxi.

Fuck it.

I wiped the sweat from my forehead and caught a driver's attention.

"Can you take me to Tunica?"

"Sure thing, boss," replied the driver in a thick Indian accent.

The taxi smelled musty, but better than halitosis.

Chuck. Poor fellow. I hope he made it to baggage claim.

The driver loaded my luggage and we headed south on Interstate 55.

CHAPTER 5

At the state line there were several police cars and emergency vehicles on the northbound side. Traffic was backed up as far down as I could see.

A big rig was laying on its side. There appeared to be a pickup truck and another car involved. A blue car, but it didn't look like my dad's. *Thank God. They must be stuck in all that traffic.*

I checked my phone, no bars. This section of the highway was notorious for dead zones, probably why they weren't answering my calls.

I looked for my dad's car. The taxi was speeding. It was hard for my eyes to catch every vehicle.

"Please slow down! I'm looking for someone in that traffic."

"Very sorry, sir."

"It's a dark blue Chevy Cavalier."

"Yes sir. Okay. I'll help you look."

"Thank you, but I'd rather you watch the road."

"Yes, of course, sir."

"Do you mind turning up the air conditioning?"

"Are you too cold?"

"No, I'm too hot."

"Of course, sir."

"There they are!"

"Excellent, sir."

"That's my dad's car!"

"Very good, sir!"

The accumulated worry ran from my mind. Peace washed over me like a cool spring waterfall.

I texted Jennifer. "Hey, baby. When u get this, turn around n come home. I couldn't get u guys, so I took a taxi. I just saw u stuck in traffic. Can't wait to see u! Love u!"

CHAPTER 6

The taxi pulled into the farm and parked between the main house and guest house below it. My parents let Jennifer live in the guest house while I was at flight school in Pensacola. She had a miserable pregnancy and I wanted her to be close to my family.

The farm had been passed down for three generations, and I supposed it would be mine one day. Dad wasn't interested in being a full-time farmer, so he rented the fields to local farmers. Corn was growing in the front fields, cotton in the rear.

I have great memories of growing up here, like riding my motorcycle all over the thousand acres and having friends over for campouts behind the barn.

I would like to leave all this to my son someday, and hopefully he will have a son to pass it on to.

I settled into the guest house and fixed a sandwich. It made me think of Chuck for a moment.

As I finished eating, I heard a car pull up the driveway.

Yes! They're here!

I ran outside.

I recognized the silver Mercedes. It was Mike Kingston, my dad's best friend and attorney. They graduated from Ole Miss together.

"Hi, Danny. Good to see you."

"You too, Mike."

"Is your dad here?"

"No. He, mom and Jennifer are stuck in traffic."

"When did you get here?"

"About an hour ago."

"Your dad said you'd be home today. You're looking good. How was flight school?"

"Demanding. Tiring. Glad to be home. I'm shipping out to the USS Enterprise in a couple weeks."

"That's great, Danny. Glad to see your childhood dreams have come true."

"Me too."

I heard a car coming up the driveway, but I couldn't see it through the tall corn.

"That must be them," I said.

The car appeared from the edge of the corn field.

What the hell?

It was the Tunica County Sheriff.

He got out and took off his hat. He knew Mike and they shook hands.

He looked at me, "Are you Danny, the one I used to chase on that motorcycle years ago?"

"Yes, sir."

What the Sheriff said next changed my life forever.

CHAPTER 7

The Sheriff looked me and frowned. "I'm awfully sorry to tell you this, son, but there was a terrible accident on I-55 today near the state line. A tractor trailer moved over quickly from the left lane and apparently didn't see the pickup truck and car beside him. It struck both vehicles and somehow they all plunged through the guardrails and over the embankment. The truck landed on the car, killing all three passengers. They were identified as Daniel Dedd III, Sofie Dedd and Jennifer Dedd."

A frigid wave blew through me. I felt the hair on my arms stand on end.

My legs could no longer support the weight of my body. I buckled slowly and curled into a fetal position.

I felt everything and nothing.

I began to shiver. My teeth rattled. I closed my eyes and pulled my knees hard into my chest.

I felt a hand on my shoulder. "I'm very sorry for your loss, son. Let me know if there's anything I can do," said the Sheriff.

I felt the earth spinning beneath me and I was falling through space. I struggled to catch my breath.

A hand gently squeezed my arm. "Danny, are you okay?" Mike asked.

I heard the Sheriff drive away.

Mike squeezed a little harder. "Danny. Talk to me, son."

I tried to speak but nothing came out.

A rogue wave of tears started near my stomach, rippled up my neck and out my eyes and nose. I opened my mouth to scream. Silence.

I didn't want to open my eyes. I saw Jennifer walking toward me, like an angel of light. Her aura filled my darkness. I wanted to taste her sweet kisses, hold her tiny hands and stroke her hair.

I reached for her. She smiled and blew a kiss as she drifted away. The darkness swallowed her light.

I heard myself shouting, "No! Don't go! Don't go!"

I vomited.

I opened my eyes to find Mike offering me a handkerchief. I wiped my mouth and he helped me sit up.

I saw his lips moving but there was no sound.

My soulmate was gone. My little Danny was dead. My parents were gone. This made no sense.

Mike sat down beside me and rested his arm on my shoulders. We sat in silence for an eternity.

"Danny, let's go up to the house, son."

I stood up with Mike's help. He embraced me.

My legs were rubber bands. It was a sluggish walk to the house.

I remembered where dad hid the house key, under a flower pot on the porch. Mike opened the door.

Money greeted us in the kitchen. He slinked around my feet, rubbing his chin on my shoes, purring. I picked him up, the sole remnant of my family. He loved Jennifer. She called him Sylvester, like the cartoon cat. His fur against my skin and the vibrations on my chest were comforting. I bet she held him this morning.

I made sure he had food and water, and then sat at the kitchen table with my forehead resting on my folded arms.

Mike made two cups of hot tea and joined me at the table. We sat for a while. I picked at the table's edge, staring at my cup, into infinity.

Mike broke the silence. "I'll call the Coroner's office and the funeral home. I'll handle all the details and arrangements."

"Thanks. Would you mind calling Robert and Judy?"

"I'll make sure they know."

I guess I knew how they would feel. I just lost a child too.

"Can I get you anything?" Mike offered.

"A pack of Marlboro Lights and a twelve pack of Yuengling would be nice."

Mike furrowed his brow, "You smoke?"

"I do now."

"So would I. I'll be right back."

CHAPTER 8

I sat on the porch swing, smoked several cigarettes and drank all the Yuengling. Mom used to scold me for going too high on this thing. Sometimes I would lie here in the evenings while mom and dad sat in those rocking chairs. I'd listen as they told stories and sipped wine.

My dad frequently offered me a drink, much to mom's chagrin. He would promptly remind her that in Germany children were permitted to drink in public when they were twelve years old - holding up his index finger - and they were not permitted to drive until they were twenty-one. He said they needed time to learn how to drink and drive, and then he'd laugh.

I loved his laugh. It started loud and then regressed into a wheezing Muttley snicker.

I caught a nasty buzz from the Yuengling. I wanted to drive my El Camino off a cliff. Maybe I'd wake up from this dream.

I took four Ibuprofen and lie down on my parents' bed. Their scent lingered there. Dad's Old Spice, mom's Gucci Rush 2.

Holy shit!

I sprinted down to the guest house.

I snatched a pillow from the bed, buried my face and inhaled Jennifer. I clutched it against my chest. One of her long brown hairs tickled my chin. I gathered several from the sheets, held them to my nostrils, eyes closed, swaying.

I yearned for the remnants of Jennifer's existence. I wanted her residue all over my body.

I went into the bathroom. Her washcloth and towel were hanging on the drying rack. I took off my clothes. The washcloth stimulated my genitals as I took deep breaths from the slightly damp towel. I could see her soaking up water droplets from her breasts and pregnant belly. And then she wrapped her hair in the towel. I held her smooth brown skin against mine.

The release came quickly, into the washcloth. I showered and used her towel.

CHAPTER 9

Two lonely weeks passed quickly, with the help of Yuengling and sleep. But it was time to go.

I landed aboard the USS Enterprise in the Persian Gulf. The Enterprise led the war on terror after 9/11. I didn't want to be there; yet this was the only family I had left.

They put me in the air right away, thinking it would take my mind off things. Reminded me of when Maverick lost Goose in Top Gun. I flew several missions into Afghanistan and Pakistan. I dropped laser-guided bombs on the Taliban in support of dislodging Osama Bin Laden. I wondered how many people I killed, or how many women and children I'd vaporized. Probably hundreds. Ironically, I had no remorse. It was just business.

We were relieved by the USS Theodore Roosevelt and set sail for Norfolk. I was unable to concentrate in meetings. I was making mistakes. The last one sent my F-14 Tomcat into the ocean. I followed in a parachute. On the way to splashdown it was eerily quiet. Just what I needed at the time.

The captain grounded me, subject to a psychological examination.

The shrink said I was not fit to fly. I was put on a desk to schedule flight plans and write procedures. I fell asleep several times.

I begged the shrink to recommend an honorable discharge. He did. And I was out. My dream was dead. And that was okay with me.

CHAPTER 10

I spent a couple months at the homestead doing nothing, sometimes contemplating suicide. At least I'd be with Jennifer. I stopped taking my Lexapro and drank a twelve pack of Yuengling daily.

I lay in my childhood bedroom, which mom had not changed since I left home. My model airplanes were still hanging from the ceiling, Rock-'n-Roll posters on the wall – U2, Def Leppard, Metallica, AC/DC, Pink Floyd. I tried to remember the first time I wanted to be a pilot. I couldn't.

The only thing that kept running through my mind was a quote from Andy Dufresne in The Shawshank Redemption, "Get busy living, or get busy dying." I wasn't going to kill myself, so I figured I should probably get busy living.

CHAPTER 11

⚜

I parked my El Camino in the front row at Poplar Business Plaza in Memphis. I was visiting Derrick Geyser, Trustee of the Dedd Family Trust, held by FT Financial, a well-respected firm in Memphis. I needed money.

Not sure who told me, but Derrick was rumored to be a big gambler, a high-roller in Vegas, with bookie connections in Memphis. I don't think dad knew this. Maybe he did. I remember him watching SEC football games and getting all excited, and in the next change of the channel he was cursing, even if it was Ole Miss winning.

I didn't have an appointment. The lady took my name and said Derrick was at lunch and would return in twenty minutes. I found a seat in the marble lobby.

Suits and skirts walked by from time to time. Some of them flashed me strange looks. This was not a place you'd normally see someone dressed like me. Maybe it was my torn jeans, U2 T-shirt, unshaven face and unkempt hair. I didn't smell good either. But not as bad as Chuck that day on the plane.

I saw a young couple walk in. They were hand in hand, smiling. She had a big diamond on her finger. He kissed her as they approached the receptionist's desk. I felt contempt.

The older man with them said he was there to see about withdrawing money to buy his son and new daughter-in-law their first home. I'm sure my dad would have done the same.

A perky short man in a dark suit with shiny shoes came out to greet them. He swung a gaze at me with furrowed brow. He was a weasel with a fake demeanor. I suspected he had short-man's syndrome. Little bastard. He escorted them through a door marked PRIVATE.

I fiddled through Time magazine for a few minutes. I heard a man say my name. It was Derrick offering a handshake. I had met him once or twice in social settings with my dad. He always had too much to drink.

I didn't want to shake his hand, so I did the fist-bump thing, which caught him off guard. By the look on his face, apparently it was too rudimentary for the setting. I blew it up like Chuck. He didn't.

Derrick was a little shorter than me, with a non-athletic build. He was wearing an expensive dark blue suit, white pressed shirt and red tie with a company logo clasp. His gray hair was thinning and he looked aged beyond fifty. His eyebrows were disheveled, broken off to stubbles in several places. Maybe he shaved them. Weird.

"Thanks for coming, Danny. Follow me."

He led me through the PRIVATE door, down a quiet hallway lined with fancy paintings. I caught a glimpse of that short man through a narrow window in his closed office door. I heard laughing. I felt a twinge of disgust.

Derrick stopped at the end of the hall. "After you, Danny."

His office smelled clean and professional. His desk was made of polished cherry wood. A high-back leather chair dominated the room.

I sat down across from him and looked out the windows behind his desk. I could see the El Camino in the parking lot. It gave me a sense of comfort.

"Danny, I'm so sorry for not making it to the funeral. I was out of town. Please accept my condolences."

I was still staring out the windows. "Thanks."

"I'm sure it's been hard. I haven't seen you since the Christmas party a few years ago, I believe."

I nodded lightly, in no mood for shallow niceties.

Derrick folded his arms on the desk, revealing a large-face Rolex and a platinum wedding band. I was raised in wealth, but my dad forbade me from promoting that type of privilege. We would not disrespect the hard work and sacrifices of our Dedd forefathers who came here from Germany and worked the soil, the same soil where I rode my motorcycle.

"What can I do for you today, Danny?"

"I'm here to set up a monthly stipend from the Trust. I'm running low on funds. I don't have much left from the military, and I put Jennifer's small life insurance into a savings account. I can't bring myself to dip into it."

"That should be no problem," he assured me. "How much do you need?"

"How much is in the trust?"

He clicked the computer mouse and hit Enter a few times. "Today, the trust has a balance of just over twenty million dollars."

"Only twenty million? I thought there was a lot more than that, especially with dad's life insurance."

Derrick's face turned red. "No offense, Danny, but your father made some bad investments, against my advice of course."

I stared at him in scorn. How dare he disrespect my dad? I resisted the urge to go over the desk and tear him a new asshole. I took a deep breath. "I need ten thousand a month, starting today."

"No problem," he said. "I'll need your bank account information."

"You already have it."

"Oh yes, here it is."

I wanted to wipe the incompetent grin off his face. "Deposit ten thousand today and every month from now on."

"Not a problem."

I tapped my index finger on the desk. "There's one more thing."

Derrick cocked his head to the side, "What's that?"

I moved to the edge of my chair. "I'm going to buy a Lear jet."

Derrick sat back in his chair and rubbed his stubby eyebrows. "How much is that going to cost?"

"Only $6.8 million."

I was delighted to watch him squirm.

"Why do you need a Lear jet?"

I spoke through gritted teeth. "It's my money."

"Yes, that's correct. But I don't want you to make the same mistakes your father made."

I looked at the El Camino, wishing I had a gun to shoot this pompous ass.

"Let me ask you a question, derelict, I mean Derrick."

His face turned red again. He gripped the armrests and I saw his knuckles turning white.

I continued in a relaxed manner. "What is the process of changing the Trustee of my Trust? Not sure FT Financial and you are working in the best interests of my heritage."

Derrick appeared to force a smile, speaking slowly. "That won't be necessary, Danny. When do you need the $6.8 million?"

A sense of satisfaction soothed whatever anger was still within me. "Today."

He hesitated with another forced grin. "Sure thing."

I wasn't done with this jerk.

"I also want to build a small runway on the homestead, and I will also need an underground fuel tank, which will require expensive permits and county approval."

Derrick fiddled with his pen. "How much will that cost?"

"Only a few hundred thousand more." I could not resist a chuckle. "But, hey, I'll still have over twelve million to get me through, right?"

Derrick leaned in toward me. "Are you sure about this, Danny? I mean, are you REALLY sure?"

I pounded my fist on the desk. It felt good. "Make it happen!"

"Okay, young man. No need to get emotional. $7.1 million. You'll have it today."

I noticed a Las Vegas coffee mug sitting on his bookshelf. I walked over and picked it up. I wanted to test the rumor about him. "You ever been to Vegas?"

"A few times. You?"

"Never."

"You a big gambler?"

"Not really."

"Then why go to Vegas? Tunica is just down the road."

"There are other things besides gambling."

"Like what?"

He would not make eye contact. He appeared to be making my transfer on the computer. "Just…things."

I couldn't believe what came out of my mouth next. There was no reason to make nice with this guy. "Maybe I'll fly us both out there when the runway is ready."

He looked at me, puzzled. "You're kidding, right?"

Crap. I have to go with this now. "Nope. I've never been there. Maybe you could show me the ropes, on the 'other things' of course."

"Not sure you could handle those 'other things,' Danny. Anyway, I just put in a transfer request for your money. Anything else?"

I couldn't resist. "Yes, just one more thing."

"What's that?"

"You got a bookie in town I can use?"

"Why?"

"The fact that you asked 'why' tells me you do."

"That's my private life. Has nothing to do with my professional life."

What a crock of shit. "Really?"

"You need to leave now. You'll have your money today. You can keep the mug."

I put the Vegas mug back on the shelf, beside a picture. "I'll get my own. Is this your family?"

"Yes."

"Cute kids. Is this your wife?"

I heard him ruffling some papers.

"Yes."

"She's kinda hot. How'd you get her?"

"Big cock."

I laughed.

I turned around to leave. He handed me a yellow Post-It note with a name and number on it. "Your dad used this guy."

I knew the answer, but I asked anyway. "For what?"

"Bookie."

CHAPTER 12

The runway was completed in a few weeks. In the mean time I earned my private pilot's license from Memphis Pilot School. No worries about passing the tests. I taught the instructor a few things.

I found the Lear jet in Pittsburgh, PA, of all places. The seller was a retired oil tycoon. He was happy that I was buying his baby.

I felt at home in the cockpit. Being in the air again was comforting, like home. I could go anywhere. Free from all that shit down there.

There was no debate on what I would name it. Her name was The Jennifer. I had it stenciled on the sides.

CHAPTER 13

I landed at the homestead and parked The Jennifer flawlessly in the barn. I kissed her nose.

Money greeted me in the kitchen. I rubbed his head. It reminded me of rubbing something for good luck, which led me to think about gambling.

I found the Post-It note from Derrick and called the number. *Why not? My dad did it.*

I opened a Yuengling and dialed the number with anticipation.

The guy answered in a deep, unwelcoming voice. "Yeah?"

"Hello," I said, a bit shaky. "I was given your number by Derrick Geyser."

"So?"

"I'd like to place a few bets."

"What's your name?"

"Danny Dedd."

"Where do you live?"

"Tunica."

"Go to the casino."

"I hate casinos. I want to bet through you."

"Don't call me, I'll call you."

Silence. I thought I lost the connection. Apparently he hung up on me. Bastard.

I chugged the rest of my Yuengling and grabbed another one from the fridge. My phone rang. It was the bookie's number. I answered in a deep, unwelcoming voice. "Yeah?"

"Derrick says you are good for a few dollars."

"More than a few."

"You ever gamble?"

"Only with my life in the Navy."

"I'll start you out with a $5,000 limit."

"I'm good for more than that."

"We'll start there."

"How does this work?"

He gave me a website address, a username and password. I'd figure it out from there.

I logged on and placed ten bets at $300 each on several sporting events. I felt like an undisciplined kid in a candy store.

I didn't bother to watch any of the events. Whatever. It's only $3,000.

I woke up the next morning. It was Friday, hopefully my lucky Friday. I logged onto the website. I lost them all. *Dammit!*

I called the bookie and asked him how to pay. We arranged a meeting for later that afternoon in the parking lot of Perkins at the corner of Poplar and Highland in Memphis. The bookie said he'd be in a white Ford Explorer. Bring cash.

I arrived early, after stopping by the bank to get the money.

The bookie pulled in slowly and parked in the back.

My El Camino didn't have air conditioning. I brought along a small cooler of Yuengling to keep me cool, yet I was soaked with sweat and nerves.

I approached the Explorer like a thief in a department store, looking around for authorities, walking inconspicuously.

The driver's window was down. I saw him staring at me in the side mirror. He had a dark complexion and short black hair.

I wasn't sure what to say. "Hi, I'm Danny." It sounded like I was greeting another boy on the playground.

He didn't make eye contact. "You got the three grand?" Yep, that was the voice on the phone.

"Right here." I handed him an envelope. He said nothing, just counting. I'm sure the teller counted it right.

He looked at me. "I tell you what, Mr. Dedd, I'll increase your line to ten grand. We'll see where that goes. But don't ever, and I mean EVER, think about screwing me."

I fought the Taliban, yet this guy made me nervous. My voice was noticeably shaky. "I understand."

I stood there contemplating. It just came out. I wasn't' sure if it was proper protocol or not. "What's your name?"

He quickly closed the window, put the Explorer in reverse and exited the parking lot. I guess he didn't want me to know his name. I stood there watching him leave, like I'd done something wrong.

During the hour drive back to Tunica I felt the effect of the Yuengling kicking in. I wanted to get back into the sky with The Jennifer. I stopped at a gas station for another six pack and some Marlboro Lights.

I sat on the porch, smoking, drinking, thinking. My buzz conjured up a terrible idea, as buzzes normally do.

I called Derrick and asked if he was ready to take the maiden voyage in The Jennifer to Las Vegas this weekend.

"Are you serious?" he replied.

"Yep. Meet me at the homestead at 7:00 a.m."

"Sounds good."

CHAPTER 14

❦

My alarm went off Saturday morning at 6:00 a.m. *Why the hell did I set it so early?* And then I remembered. *Oh, fuck! Derrick. Vegas. Shit!* Damn buzz. I resolved to make the best of it. At least I will get to fly The Jennifer.

I filed a flight plan and fixed half a peanut butter sandwich and a glass of water. I let Money lick some peanut butter off my finger. I loaded his food and water bowls. "I'll only be gone a little while, buddy." He purred as I rubbed his chin.

In the barn, I finished inspecting every inch of The Jennifer when I heard a car pull up. It was Derrick with a suit case and bottle of champagne.

He acted like we were best friends. *Dammit!* I suppose it was his excitement for Vegas. I just played along. My excitement was in the flying, not the destination.

Derrick popped the cork and took a few swigs. I lifted the bottle to Heaven and loudly dedicated the plane to Jennifer, little Danny and my parents.

Derrick grabbed it from me and chugged it empty. He then yelled, "I Christen thee…The Jennifer!" He smashed it on her nose.

I was irritated. "I was supposed to do that."

He looked at me, apparently unsure of whether he should apologize. "Uh, sorry, I'm just excited about Vegas."

He acted a bit immature for a fifty-something. I wasn't sure if I should punch him or have pity. I can't believe this guy is in charge of my money.

We boarded, and for the next ten minutes I went through my checklist as Derrick grew impatient. I had to explain that this wasn't a car, "you don't just jump in, start it up and go. There are procedures to follow, unless you want to die."

He appeared to be ignorant of such things. "My apologies, Danny. Again, just excited. I can appreciate your diligence. Let's hope for a smooth flight."

"Don't worry," I replied, "I checked the entire flight path to Las Vegas this morning. Light winds and sparse clouds the entire way."

"Nice!"

I taxied The Jennifer out of the barn and onto the runway. With no hesitation, I pushed full throttle up. She wasn't a Tomcat, but I still loved that feeling of being sucked into my seat with engines roaring.

"Holy shit!" Derrick shouted. "This is fucking incredible! Better than a goddamn roller coaster!"

I decided to have some fun, and maybe get Derrick to shit his pants. I pulled back on the stick, airborn, steep slope, and then pushed into a hard left turn.

I caught a glance at Derrick. He struggled to keep his head straight. I jerked the stick quickly leftward, causing his head to tap on the fuselage.

"I think I'm gonna throw up," he mumbled.

I laughed. The Jennifer was in a full perpendicular left bank, pulling what felt to me like two G's. I was feeling light headed, so I took a deep breath and held it hard to push blood to my head.

I leveled her out in a straight line toward the house, and then pushed down on the stick, which I'm sure lifted Derrick's stomach into his chest. He looked a bit pale. I buzzed the house at less than fifty feet.

"How 'bout that!" I shouted.

Derrick could barely speak. "You goddamn nut."

"Hell," I said, "that was nothing compared to what I did in the Navy."

Satisfied, I pointed her westward.

Derrick shook his head like a dog after a bath, "I thought we were going to crash into the house."

I chuckled. That felt good.

CHAPTER 15

The four-hour flight was smooth, as expected. McCarran International Airport was busy, but it was nice to not have to deal with the crowds. We took our bags for a short walk to ground transportation. Derrick hailed a taxi and instructed the driver to take us to the Wynn Hotel.

The lobby at the Wynn was lined with Italian marble. I asked the bellhop what I was smelling. "White passion tea aroma, sir. They pump it into the air here," he replied.

I filled my lungs several times. It was soothing.

We stepped into a long line of waiting guests. One of the girls at the front desk caught my eye. For some reason she wasn't checking in anyone, just standing there plucking on her keyboard. She looked like Jennifer. Long, soft brown hair, smooth skin with a perfect tan pigment, dark eyes and small lips. She wore black framed glasses that gave her a slightly nerdy appearance, and she had a faint mole on her upper lip. Her dark blue suit with soft beige pinstripes gave her a touch of professional elegance.

I saw a lady near the casino entrance screaming at a slot machine. People were giving her high fives. Must have been a hell of a win. Slot machines chimed as far as I could see down both sides of the wide aisle. I felt a tug on my shirt. "Let's go, Danny," Derrick insisted.

We skipped in front of everyone in line. Very odd. Derrick led me to the girl who looked like Jennifer. There was a gold sign sitting on the counter in front of her: Platinum Members Only. According to her name tag, she was Sarah from Grove City, Pennsylvania, wherever the hell that was.

Derrick pulled out his American Express. "Here you go, sweetheart." She smiled, but I don't think she wanted to.

Derrick winked at me, like I should be impressed. Sarah ran the card and asked Derrick to sign. I saw him wink at her. I could tell she wasn't pleased, but remained professional. She spoke to someone on the phone with a sweet voice, "Mr. Geyser is here, sir."

A few minutes later a classy looking man wearing an expensive suite appeared from a door behind the counter. He greeted Derrick like he was the most important guest in the hotel. The man motioned for a bellhop to carry our bags. He escorted us to the elevator and pushed floor 25.

Derrick looked at me and winked again. "Not everyone gets to stay on the twenty-fifth floor, Danny boy." I didn't react. I was more concerned than impressed. I wondered if my trust fund really had millions in it.

We entered room 2507, a magnificent suite with marble throughout. Two large pillars greeted us in the foyer, which led into a great sitting room with dark leather furniture.

The man promptly excused the bellhop. Derrick and he spent a few minutes in private conversation. I took this opportunity to stroll through the suite.

The kitchen countertops were granite. It was good to see a stocked fridge and wet bar. The four bedrooms were spacious, with stand-up showers and whirlpool bathtubs. The outside wall in the sitting room was made of glass with a breathtaking view of the busy strip. I wondered why we would need all this for two guys for two days.

I saw Derrick give the man what looked like a sizeable tip. The man bowed slightly, thanked Derrick, and promised to take care of our needs during the visit.

Derrick shut the door. "Well, buddy, wutta-ya think of this place?"

"Very posh," I said. "How did you manage this?"

He furrowed his brow, "Let's just say I've been here before."

"I suspected as much."

Derrick poured two Crown Royals on the rocks and invited me to sit. He assured me that the next two days would be full of booze, gambling and women.

"Women?"

"Yes. Women. You know, those things with tits and vaginas."

"I thought you were happily married."

"I am. But like they say, 'What happens in Vegas stays in Vegas!'"

What did my father see in this guy?

"Listen, Derrick, I'm in for the booze and gambling. But the women...no. Count me out."

"Okay, Danny, I know you just lost the love of your life a few months ago. I can understand that. But you've gotta get back on that horse someday."

Derrick had a way of rousing my anger. I wanted to knock him out, bind his limbs and stuff him in the closet for the next two days.

I cut my eyes at him. "Not interested."

"Not a problem, Danny. I'm having a call girl or two in the room tonight. I like to ride as many horses as I can." He laughed and took a swig of Crown Royal.

I dismissed his smugness. "You paid for the room. Do whatever you want."

He pointed at me, like everything was fine. "Time to gamble, Danny boy!"

CHAPTER 16

‹❈›

We both showered and I fixed some sandwiches, a fond reminder of Chuck.

"Do you play poker?" Derrick asked.

"No. I'm a slot kind of guy."

He laughed. "I like slots too…and sluts."

We made it to the casino floor. Derrick made a bee line for the poker tables. "Come find me when you're ready to leave. I'll be winning big at a poker table somewhere."

Finally, a reprieve from this jerk. "Okay."

I walked around for a few minutes and found an empty Miss Kitty machine. A waitress, whose breasts I could not ignore, strolled by shouting "Cocktails!"

I raised a finger, "I'll have a Yuengling."

"A what?"

"A Yuengling."

"What's a yingling, sweety?"

"It's a beer."

"Sorry honey. No yingling."

I pursed my lips. "Damn. Uh. How about a Corona with a lime?"

"Sure thing, sweetie."

I loaded Miss Kitty with a hundred dollars and played max bet, which was two dollars and fifty cents per spin. I blew through it in fifteen minutes and decided to throw in another hundred.

A young lady sat down beside me to play the Buffalo machine. She smelled good. I took a quick peek. It was Sarah. I looked back at her and held my gaze. I felt my heart swell. She could be Jennifer's twin.

She smiled at me. "Didn't I just see you at the front desk?"

I couldn't believe she remembered me. I had to tell myself to speak. "Uhh, yes, that was me."

"Thought so," she said, touching my arm.

"Are employees allowed to gamble?" I asked.

She chuckled, "There are no rules against it when we're off the clock."

"That's cool. This is quite a coincidence, don't you think?"

"What do you mean?" she replied.

"Well, I just saw you behind the counter, and now you are sitting here beside me. If I didn't know better, I'd think you were stalking me."

She laughed, "Stalking you? Really? For shame, sir. This is just pure luck. After all, we ARE in a casino."

I didn't want to, but I turned my attention back to Miss Kitty. On my seventh spin I hit the bonus for eight hundred seventy seven dollars. "Yes!"

She gave me a high five. "Awesome, dude!"

"Thanks. I guess I have a way with kitties."

She winked at me. "Oh, do you now?"

I wasn't sure how to react to that. I extended my hand. "I'm Danny."

"I'm Sarah."

I pointed to her name tag. "I know."

The waitress delivered my Corona. I looked at Sarah, "What would you like to drink?"

"I'm good."

"You sure?"

"Yep. Thanks anyway."

We played together for two hours, which seemed like five minutes. I found out where Grove City, Pennsylvania was. I never spoke of Jennifer or what happened. I didn't want Sarah to feel sorry for me, and I didn't want her to think she was some kind of rebound. I just told her that I lived in Mississippi and was recently discharged from the Navy. I was in Vegas to relax for a couple days.

I wasn't hungry, but I wanted to spend more time with her. "Can I treat you to dinner?"

"I'd love to," she replied, "but I have a job at another casino. Starts in an hour. I really need to leave."

Shit.

She took a small piece of paper from her purse, wrote on it and handed it to me. "Call me," she said.

"I will," I said, grinning ear to ear.

CHAPTER 17

I found Derrick sitting at a three-card poker table, highly intoxicated. I tapped him on the shoulder. His speech was slurred. "I juss loss ten grand, Danny boy!"

"Derrick, you've had enough to drink and you've lost too much money. We need to leave."

"Lissen, you young fuck, you don't tell me when I've had enough to drink."

I looked at the dealer, "He's done, sir. We have to go."

The dealer nodded, "Probably a good idea, sir."

"Danny boy! Less go play some sluts!"

"No more gambling for you tonight. Let's go."

He leaned in close to whisper. The alcohol stench was unbearable. "I don't mean gambling. I mean poosee. I want some poosee, Danny boy."

I had to laugh. "You probably can't get it up right now. No 'poosee' for you."

"I'll be aaaight. Juss get me to the room."

CHAPTER 18

Derrick leaned on the elevator wall, rifting.

If this bastard pukes, I'm going to leave him lying in it. "Don't puke, Derrick. Breathe."

He took a few breaths. "I'll be aaaight. I don't puke."

He held up his fist for a bump. I ignored it. The twenty fifth floor could not come soon enough.

I helped him into his bed and put a garbage can next to it. "Derrick, use this garbage can if you have to puke. You are in your bedroom."

"I told you, I don't puke!"

I wanted to smother him with a pillow and say he died in his sleep. "You stay here, Derrick. I'm going to take a shower. I smell like smoke."

"Have fun! Don't play with it too hard!"

I flipped him the bird on the way out.

"Hey, that's mean!" he shouted.

I finished my shower, put on blue jeans and a Metallica T-shirt, and went to the refrigerator to look for a bottle of water. I was interrupted by a knock at the door.

I yelled toward Derrick's bedroom, "Derrick, you expecting someone?"

No answer.

I went to the door and peeked through the peephole. Two made-up ladies were standing there. They looked distorted in the peephole. I couldn't tell if they were attractive or not. One of them knocked again.

I opened the door, "May I help you, ladies?"

"Are you Derrick?" one of them said, chewing the crap out of a piece of gum, "I sure hope you are. Holy shit, you're hot."

Typical hookers in short, tight dresses and stiletto heels; they looked better through the peephole. "Uhhhh...no...I'm...yeah, never mind. Derrick is in the bedroom."

"Oh hell," said the other woman, "I hope he's half as hot as you are."

I escorted them to Derrick's bedroom. The first lady turned to me and ran her finger down my chest, "Wanna join us?"

"No thanks, ma'am. I'm good."

"I bet you are," she said, staring at me as she slowly closed the door.

I heard rustling and laughing, so I turned on the TV, loud.

I leaned back on the couch. My mind drifted to Sarah, making comparisons to Jennifer. Thoughts of betrayal crept in. Feelings of guilt arrived. *But she's gone. Would she want me to move on?* The struggle was overwhelming. I fell asleep.

I think I slept for at least an hour. A slamming door startled me awake. I noticed the TV was turned off. Derrick, naked, was locking the main door, holding the bottle of Crown Royal.

He strutted over to me, gripping his penis, shaking it proudly, "How 'bout that buddy? How 'bout that?"

I wanted to leave.

Derrick took a swig from the bottle. "You could have had some of that, buddy!"

I covered my face with both hands, "And you're the guy taking care of my money."

"Awww, Danny boy, you gotta have fun sometimes. Life ain't all business, bro!"

I looked at him with disgust. "First of all, I'm not your bro. Secondly, this isn't the kind of fun I like to have. Go put some clothes on."

The next two days were much the same, babysitting a megalomaniac. I was able to talk to Sarah a few times, wanting to meet up with her, but her work had gotten in the way.

She was unexpectedly invading my mind, cultivating a fresh passion, mixed with thoughts of infidelity toward Jennifer. I wanted to believe Sarah represented a new beginning, not unfaithfulness.

Sunday evening, Derrick and I flew home through clear skies. There was little conversation, which was fine with me. Derrick reminded me several times that whatever happened in Vegas stayed in Vegas. I didn't respond.

The Jennifer touched down flawlessly. I taxied her into the barn under a warm, starry sky. The engines were barely stopped when I opened the door and let Derrick out.

"See ya later, buddy," he said, with his suit case in tow. I didn't respond.

I walked to the house thinking about Sarah.

CHAPTER 19

Money greeted me at the door. He rubbed against my legs, purring, and then sprinted three slippery laps on the tile floor around the island. He skidded to a temporary halt, looked at me, meowed, and then dashed into the living room to tackle his Bear-Bear.

Mom bought him a large teddy bear when he was a kitten, and Bear-Bear has been his buddy ever since. He cleaned it regularly, slept on it, bit it, scratched it, made biscuits, and often pulled it around the house by the tail.

Jennifer loved Money. When she visited on breaks from Ole Miss she would often say she couldn't wait to see Money. She taught him to play fetch with a toy mouse. She'd also throw pieces of his food across the kitchen floor and he'd pounce on them like prey and gobble them up. Mom noticed that Money ignored Bear-Bear when Jennifer was around. He followed Jennifer around the house and slept with her every night. She would play hide-and-seek with him. He would scurry around the house trying to find her. I could still hear her laughter echoing through the house when Money finally found her.

I filled Money's bowls with food and water, scooped the litter box, grabbed a Yuengling from the fridge and went into the living room to lie on the couch. Money jumped onto my chest, making biscuits and purring. I rubbed his chin, "You miss her too, don't you buddy?" He meowed and jumped to the floor.

Out of nowhere a gob of hopeless sludge filled me. I felt like crying, but couldn't. I grasped at some future hope, but it was like trying to catch fog. My give-a-shit was fading fast, oozing down a dark, empty, hell-filled corridor. My demons were wrestling with my angles, and winning. I was struggling to come to grips with Jennifer's absence.

I took a drink of beer, and then another, trying to drown the misery.

My gloom was interrupted by something dropping lightly onto my chest. Money was on the back of the couch looking down at me, wanting to play fetch with the toy mouse. I threw it into the kitchen, just like Jennifer used to do. Money brought it back and dropped it onto my chest again. We did this several times until I grew weary and hid it under my pillow. Money sat on the back of the couch for a few minutes and then jumped to the floor, apparently sad.

"I'm sorry, buddy. I'm just not myself anymore."

He meowed and skulked into the kitchen.

I finished the beer, rolled over and screamed into my pillow. I couldn't stop the tears from flowing.

CHAPTER 20

I woke up Monday morning on a soaked pillow, stomach growling. I opened a can of Chunky Sirloin Burger soup and had a Yuengling. I turned on the small TV in the kitchen and watched ESPN while I ate. Money rubbed against my legs. I put a dab of soup on my finger and he licked it clean. Watching ESPN tempted me to do more betting.

I fired up the computer and logged into the website. I had a ten-thousand dollar credit line to play with now. There were always plenty of games and horse races to bet on. I placed several small wagers on long shots, and then placed a mother-load on some horse named Blue Winged Flyer. Cool name for a horse. I watched the race online. Blue got off to a slow start out of the gates, but came around the final turn in first place. The jockey was whipping the shit out of Blue, who started to fade about fifty yards from the finish line. Seventh place. "Just my fucking luck!" I shouted. "I couldn't win a goddamn turd from a toilet bowl!"

I called the bookie and arranged another meeting at Perkins.

"When can you meet?" he asked.

"I can be there in two hours."

"See you there," the bookie replied.

I only had a few thousand cash at the house. I needed to stop by the bank to get the rest. On my way to the bank I called Derrick.

"I need you to wire ten thousand to my account."

"Why?" Derrick asked.

"Doesn't matter."

"Yes it does, Danny. I'm in charge of your Trust, including making sure you don't spend it frivolously."

"What? Really? Someone who loses ten grand at a poker table has no right to judge how I spend my money!"

"Danny, this has nothing to do with Vegas. I just...."

"Transfer the goddamn money, Derrick!"

"Okay. I'm just telling you. If you start blowing your money, I have an obligation to intercede on behalf of the Trust."

"Noted. Transfer the money."

"You'll have it in twenty minutes."

I pulled into the drive-thru at the First Tennessee Bank branch across from Methodist Hospital on Union Avenue. I put my driver's license in the canister and pushed the button to send it to the teller.

A young female voice came through the speaker, "What can I do for you today, Mr. Dedd?"

"I need ten thousand cash, all hundreds please."

"Sir," said the teller, "I'll need two forms of I.D. for this size of transaction."

I felt put off. I frequented this branch often and knew several employees there, but I didn't recognize this teller. "Is Kibbles 'n Bits working today?" I asked.

"Excuse me, sir?" said the teller.

"Kibbles 'n Bits."

"I'm sorry, sir. I don't know any Kibbles 'n Bits."

I laughed, "Gary Kibble."

"Oh, Gary. Yes. One moment, sir."

The teller left the window. I tapped my index finger on the steering wheel, then wiped the sweat from my forehead.

"Hey, Danny!" Gary said through the speaker.

"Hi, Kibble! How's Bits?"

Gary laughed, "Hungry as a dog!"

"Better feed him then!"

"You know I will!" he replied.

Gary came out of the closet to me a few years ago. Not sure why he chose to do that with me. It wasn't like we were best friends or anything. I was just a bank customer. I already suspected it and didn't care if he was gay or not. He wrote his name GArY on a piece of paper and slid it to me across the teller window. I looked at it and said, "I know. No big deal." And with that, the Kibbles-N-Bits routine was born.

"Listen, Gary, I need ten thousand from my account, but she is asking for two forms of I.D. Can you vouch for me?"

"Of course!"

I saw Gary talking to the teller, and then he gave me a thumbs up. I returned the gesture. I think he's hot for me, but I'm not bent that way. Nonetheless, I think he's a cool guy.

"Sorry about that, Mr. Dedd," said the teller.

"No worries. You must be new here."

"Yes. I'm sure I'll know you next time, Mr. Dedd. There is one small problem though."

"What's that?"

"You only have nine thousand in the account."

"What? There should be another ten thousand…"

"Well," she interrupted, "I see a ten thousand dollar wire that just came in. One moment, please."

I watched her conferring with Gary, and then she came back to the window. "No worries. All hundreds, Mr. Dedd?"

"Yes, please."

I took the envelope from the canister and exited the drive-thru.

I pulled into the parking lot at Perkins and saw the bookie's white Ford Explorer parked in the back row. I walked up to the open window and handed him an envelope.

He counted it quickly and then looked at me, like it wasn't all there, but I know it was. "You still want to know my name?"

"Sure."

"Joseph. Not Joe. Not Joey. Joseph."

"Got it, Joseph. Since I think I've proven myself to you, can I have a credit line of fifty thousand?"

"Sure."

"Really?"

"I said sure, didn't I?"

"I thought you would give me some flack about it."

"I know you're good for it, Mr. Trust Fund Baby. Ten thousand was just to test your character. Fifty is no problem now."

"You know I'll never screw you, right?"

"You better not."

"Can I ask you a question, Joseph?"

"Sure."

"Does Derrick lose a lot?"

"Good luck, Danny." The bookie rolled up his window and drove away.

CHAPTER 21

I thought about Sarah during the drive home: her sweet, tantalizing aroma; her brown skin like Jennifer's; her sexy glasses; the way she talked.

I felt a crotch tingle without pangs of infidelity. *Progress.* I decided to wait until I got home to call her. I was enjoying the Kurt and Rod show on the radio. *This is the Kurt and Rod Show! We hang out on the air!*

I called Sarah as soon as I got home. We talked for an hour before she said she had to get ready for work. I told her to skip work and keep talking to me late into the night. She laughed, "I really wish I could."

"Well," I said, "maybe I'll just fly out there to see you."

"Really?"

"Absolutely."

"I'd like that. When?"

"How about tonight?"

"A plane ticket would be really expensive on such short notice."

I laughed, "People who have their own planes don't need tickets."

"Yeah, right."

"I'm not kidding. I have my own plane. I could be there tonight if you want."

"Well," she replied, "I do want, but I have to work. This weekend would be awesome though. You really have your own plane?"

"Yep."

"Seriously?"

"Yep."

"I'll make you a deal then. If you promise to be here tonight, I'll blow off work."

"Deal!"

"I still don't believe you. I'll be at the airport in five hours. If you're not there, I'm leaving, and you owe me a day's pay."

"You're on!"

CHAPTER 22

The four-hour flight had light turbulence, but nothing to complain about. I landed in Vegas and called Sarah. She was waiting in the cell phone lot and could pick me up in a few minutes.

"Look for the really cute girl in a pink VW Beetle," she said.

"Okay," I laughed, "but what are YOU driving?"

"Knucklehead. Just look for me."

Sarah arrived at the curb. I saw a pink flower propped in the dash vase and a pink ladybug ornament hanging from the mirror. The interior smelled fresh and clean.

"Pink Bug? Really?"

She ignored my questioning. "You've got some explaining to do, Danny."

"What?"

"What do you mean 'What'? Your own plane? Are you kidding me? You seemed like this unpretentious commoner at the casino. What's your story?"

"Well, I come from a wealthy family. A humble, grateful, UNPRETENTIOUS, wealthy family. My great-grandfather was a

German immigrant from Kelheim, Bavaria, and very good at making and saving a dollar. We Dedd men ever since have been faithful to his hard work, dedicating all we do to his honor."

"That's cool," she replied. "I'm glad you didn't tell me before that you had money. Don't want you to think I'm a gold digger or anything like that."

"That's why I didn't tell you. I want you to like me for me, not for what I have. Do you still like me?"

Sarah peered over the top of her glasses, "Of course I do, knucklehead."

"Drive," I insisted. "I know a great place I want to take you for dinner."

We arrived at a cozy German restaurant in the basement of a building off the beaten path, with self-seating and a live piano player who was taking requests. Derrick told me about this place. There was a giant wine-glass shaped container sitting on top of the piano for tips. I threw in a twenty and requested *Piano Man* by Billy Joel. The pianist played and sang an impeccable rendition. I leaned on the piano until the song ended.

Sarah stood beside me, stroking my back. She smelled so good. I was tingling. She took my hand and led me to a table. She insisted I sit beside her, not across the table.

She stared into my eyes, "I can't believe I was talking to you on the phone a few hours ago and now you're here."

I breathed on my fingernails and rubbed them on the front of my shirt, "Well, ya know…."

She rested her head on my shoulder. "Is this a dream?"

"Ummm…I don't think so. But it sure feels like it."

"I missed you so much," she said, "and I'm so happy you are here."

"Me too."

"I'm so sorry I have to work so much. It's not like I am trying to avoid you. I need to pay the bills, ya know?"

"I understand. Let's just focus on us tonight. No work. Just us. Deal?"

"Deal. Do you feel special?" she asked.

"Special?"

"Yes, special. I've never skipped work for a man before. You should feel special."

"Well, Miss Sarah, I DO feel special. Thank you for skipping work for little old me."

"But, of course!"

"Good evening! May I tell you about our specials tonight?" said an overbearingly happy waiter with a lisp.

"Sure," I said. He reminded me of GArY.

"Tonight we have a Jagerschnitzel, which consists of pork cutlets pounded thin, breaded and fried, then topped with a sour cream and mushroom gravy."

"I like pork pounded thin," I interrupted.

The waiter chuckled and dismissed my comment with the wave of a limp wrist.

"Stop it, you knucklehead!" Sarah said. "Let him finish."

"Sorry," I said, looking at the waiter. "Please, continue."

"Thank you, sir. I like pork too...but I digress. Anyway," he snickered, "we also have a delectable Wiener Schnitzel, which is basically a pounded thin veal with a bread crumb crust, fried in extra virgin olive oil."

"Ha, ha!" I said, looking at Sarah, "He said virgin!"

"STOP IT!" Sarah said, slapping me on the shoulder.

"I know, sir," said the waiter, "we get that a lot here."

"I like this guy." I said, pointing at the waiter.

"And for dessert," he said, "we have an authentic German cheesecake made with Quark, a soft, un-ripened German cheese, topped with Fettal Brows."

"Fettal Brows?" I asked.

"Yes," said the waiter, winking at Sarah, "Moose eyebrows deep fried in Amish butter."

I laughed.

"May I start you with some drinks?"

"I'll have a Yuengling. Tell me you have Yuengling."

"Yes, sir. We have Yuengling. But may I suggest something similar straight from the barrels of Germany?"

"Yes, of course." I replied, pretending proper etiquette.

"It's called Erdinger. A fine light lager imported directly from the homeland."

"Sounds stupendous. I'll try that."

"And for you ma'am?"

"I'll have a glass of Stemmari."

"Very well," replied the waiter.

"I can't believe you!" Sarah said as the waiter walked away.

"What?"

"All those sexual innuendoes. In front of a stranger. Really?"

"It's just who I am, darling. Get used to it."

"Don't worry, baby, I'm all in with you. Sexual innuendoes and all."

I smiled while caressing her cheek with the back of my hand. "Cool."

"Yeah," she replied, "cool."

The waiter returned quickly with our drinks. "Ready to order?"

"Yes," I said, "we'll share the Jagerschnitzel and a piece of that Quark cheesecake."

"Excellent choice," replied the waiter.

We enjoyed the Jagerschnitzel and cheesecake together, with one fork.

"Gosh, I'm full." Sarah said.

"Me too." I replied. "What's next?"

"Let's just take it as it comes," she suggested.

"I like that," I replied. "Let's crawl into that pink bug of yours and see where it takes us."

"I know a place," she said softly.

CHAPTER 23

The pink bug pulled into an apartment complex just off the strip. We took the elevator to the sixth floor. Sarah unlocked her apartment door, took me by the hand and announced that it wasn't much but it was home.

It was neat, clean and eclectic. Green lamps with two-tier shades from the '70's sat on end tables at each end of a burnt orange couch. A glass coffee table rested on a faded Persian rug. A turntable sat in the corner with LP's stacked perfectly beside it. A lava lamp in full movement sat on a small eat-in kitchen table. There were family photos and colorful artwork on the walls. I complimented the place and asked why there was no pink.

"All my pink is in there," she said, pointing to a door off the living room. "You wanna see it?"

"You know I do."

She took my hand and pulled me into her bedroom. She mashed the light switch to reveal an entire bedroom of pink – pink curtains, pink carpet, pink furniture, pink bedding, pink walls and a poster of Pink Floyd on the wall.

"I love Pink Floyd," I said. "I have one of those posters too."

"Yeah, well, I hate their music, but love the name."

"What? HATE their music? That's treason!"

She slapped my arm. "Deal with it, dude."

"So, what's your favorite color?" I asked.

"BLUE!" she responded, laughing.

I could not resist what I was feeling. I leaned my lips into her.

She put two fingers against my mouth, "You sure you wanna do this?"

"I flew four hours to see you. What do you think?"

She leaned in to kiss me. I closed my eyes and felt her soft lips on mine. I felt her dainty hands on my cheeks. And then I remembered that I didn't have any condoms.

"It's okay," she said. "I'm on the pill."

Relieved, I pulled her into me, massaging gently the small of her back. She moaned and thrust her hips into me. The taste of her kisses reminded me of Jennifer. My heart was beating through my chest. Her tongue was invading all the spaces of my mouth.

She paused and backed away. Was she having second thoughts? She stroked her hair back, removed her glasses and tossed them on the dresser behind me.

Her hands made their way to my belt, undoing it, and she asked me if that was okay. I nodded - of course it was.

She slowly slid my pants to the floor and I stepped out of them, conscious of my bulging boxers. Her attention came running back to my lips.

I clutched the bottom of her shirt and pulled it over her head, letting it drop to the floor. I quickly moved to her bra. I struggled getting it unhooked and feared it would ruin the moment. She pulled my hands away, removed the bra quickly and flung it across the room. "There," she said, "now that that's out of the way…"

She worked my shirt up slowly, kissing my stomach, then my chest. I pulled it off quickly and threw it to the floor. "There," I said, "now that that's out of the way…" She smiled, took my hands and placed them on her breasts.

I cupped them gently. They were so firm, so young. I ran my tongue gently around their hard nipples. So beautiful, smooth, and perky.

I worked my way around the side of her left breast and was turned off by an unsightly mole. It was the size of a dime, with a stiff, black hair growing out of it. I'm not sure if she was aware that I avoided it with my tongue.

Jennifer had no moles. Her body was perfect.

Sarah got on her knees and pulled my boxers to my ankles. I kicked them away with one foot. My erection had subsided slightly because of the mole, but she took care of that.

Her right hand stroked slowly as her tongue found its way around. I felt her left hand gently lift my scrotum, sending waves of relaxation through my body. I was at full attention as her strokes intensified. I heard and felt her wet mouth and hands working hard to please me.

I could not contain a whimper, which seemed to make her work even harder, like she was nearing a finish line.

I did not want to cross it yet. I pulled her up.

She seemed disappointed. "What's wrong, baby?"

I smiled and pulled her mouth onto mine, and gradually guided her to the foot of the bed.

She laid back, touching herself under her pink panties. I bent down and pulled them off. She was perfectly trimmed with a single stripe.

My tongue found her naval. She pushed on the top of my head, wanting me to go lower, which I was more than willing to do.

My tongue wasted no time circling her clitoris. It perked up as I held it with my lips, teasing it with my tongue.

She squirmed and moaned, gyrating her hips. She felt hot and wet as my thumb explored inside her.

She caressed her breasts feverishly as her breathing intensified. She squealed, "Fuck me! Oh my god, fuck me!"

I ignored her request and continued ramping up the stimulation.

She took two fistfuls of my hair and pulled me up. "Put that delicious cock inside me right now!"

She kissed me frantically while her hand tried to guide me into her.

My insertion was calculated, in small intervals. Her body bowed up in shivers. She lifted her knees and screamed, "Fuck me hard, baby! I want it all!"

I enjoyed leaving her in want. She was like a caged lioness who hadn't eaten in a week. She clawed at my back, but I ignored the pain. I gradually increased the pace and depth.

I kissed her neck, working my way around to suck her earlobe. She bit my shoulder, a little too hard, but that was okay.

We found a perfect rhythm, one that I had achieved many times with Jennifer. It was like standing in a heated waterfall, closing your eyes and becoming one with its natural beat.

Her eyes were watery. She was staring at me, through me it seemed.

She closed her eyes and announced that she was there. I wanted to go with her, so I increased my pace. Our simultaneous crescendo was deafening.

"Are you kidding me?" she shouted, tears dripping from the corners of her eyes. "That was otherworldly! I didn't know that even existed!"

"Oh my god!" I yelled at the height of orgasm. "I love you!"

I wish I hadn't said that, but a man in the throes of climax can't resist.

We lay naked, facing each other, smiling. I asked why she was crying.

"I'm happy for the first time in a very long time."

I stroked her hair, "You are so beautiful, Sarah."

"Thank you," she replied, barely able to speak. "Don't leave me."

"I'm not going anywhere tonight."

"No, I mean NEVER leave me."

"What are you getting at?"

"What I felt tonight was more real than life itself, Danny. I don't' ever want this to go away. Do you understand?"

She reminded me of what Jennifer once said: "Time isn't a factor when you love someone. When it's right, it's right." The problem was, I knew immediately it was right with Jennifer, but with Sarah it felt more like an infatuated dream, one that I could escape just by waking up and walking away.

Nonetheless. "Yes," I said. "I understand."

She placed her hand on my cheek. "I know this might sound crazy, but...."

I knew what she was going to say, since I just opened that door. I shouldn't let her say it.

She took a deep breath. "I just want to say, I love you too."

I didn't want to say it again, not under these circumstances, removed from the rush of orgasm, but it just fell off my tongue. It might have been a subconscious effort to keep her away from other men, because I surely didn't want anyone else to have her. "I love you too."

She leaped onto her knees. The mole was visible. I regretted saying the L word. "I love you, Danny. I love you, I love you, I love you! God, it is so liberating to be able to say that again. And I'm so glad you said it first. I didn't want to scare you away with that!"

I smiled, but didn't say it again. She was apparently too excited to notice. She leaned over to kiss me. I pulled her onto me, wondering what the hell just happened.

She sat on my stomach. "I want to have babies with you, Danny." She covered her mouth, "I'm sorry, is that too much, too fast?"

I wanted to say "yes." Not sure why I couldn't. I muttered the first thing that came to mind, "I like babies." *Damn tongue! You Judas!*

I didn't want to marry this girl, but I sure didn't want to lose her either.

She kissed me and whispered, "Let's move in together."

Holy shit! What do I do now?

My Judas tongue took over the situation. "Move back to Mississippi with me." I listened to what I was saying like it was another person speaking. I convinced myself that I could just kick her out if the situation turned sour.

She smiled. "Are you serious?"

I wasn't sure what to say. My betraying tongue was serious, but I wasn't. I tried to dissuade her. "What about your life here? Your jobs? Your friends? You can't just uproot overnight."

"Yes, I can. Being with you is the most important thing in my life."

I was beginning to wonder if this was all about my money, a trap. Maybe she is a gold digger. I needed to unwind this whole thing. "I wouldn't want you to go back with me and then not like it there. You would blame me for your unhappiness."

"Don't you worry about that, Mr. Dedd. This isn't some teenage crush. Love will help us work through anything."

My tongue betrayed me again. "I guess you're right." No turning back now.

The next morning we arranged for her apartment to be packed up and moved to Mississippi, including the Beetle. I told her I'd buy out her lease and pay for the move.

She packed the bare essentials for the flight back home.

CHAPTER 24

Sarah sat with me in the cockpit. I didn't talk much, and I think she grew weary of that. Apparently she saw the name on the side of the plane.

"Why do you call it 'The Jennifer'?" she asked.

I was caught a little off guard. "Old girlfriend," I said.

"Oh."

She curled up in the co-pilot seat and fell asleep. I contemplated telling her about Jennifer. If I told her now and she thinks she's just a rebound, I could turn around and take her back to Vegas. Might be my way out of this.

She awoke from her nap and went to the bathroom. She came back with a drink and kissed me on the neck, returning to the co-pilot seat. I said nothing.

She broke the silence after a few minutes. "How long until we land?"

"About an hour."

"Are you okay?"

"I have something important to tell you."

"You can tell me anything, Danny."

I told her about Ole Miss when I first met Jennifer, went into detail about our relationship, my military career, and how I went off to war. I cried as I told her how my family died in the car accident. I didn't mean to cry.

She laid her head on my arm, "I'm so sorry for your loss, Danny."

I wiped my tears. "Thank you."

"I'm here for you, baby. I'll take care of you."

She never broached the subject of being a rebound. I was disappointed, but my logical mind was working hard trying to convince me that this might work out. But my heart was not there. Nobody can replace Jennifer.

We touched down at the homestead. I parked The Jennifer in the barn and escorted Sarah to the house. She was amazed at the size of it.

I introduced her to Money. He hissed at her when she tried to pet him. I explained that it might take some time for him to adjust to her. He was not used to strangers.

"You hungry?" I asked.

"Yes."

"Is soup okay?"

"Yes." she replied, sitting down at the kitchen table.

I showed her a can of soup. "Chunky Sirloin Burger, okay with you?"

"My favorite!"

"Cool."

I put the soup in a pot and turned on the stove. "Do you mind watching this while I go into the den and fire up the computer?"

"Not at all."

I logged into the gambling website and saw the fifty-thousand dollar credit line. I did some quick research on upcoming horse races and decided to bet it all on a horse named Triple Lindy's Diver. Apparently the horse's owner was a fan of the movie *Back To School*. I snickered as I placed the bet. *This better be a good one.*

"Time to eat!" Sarah shouted.

I logged off in anticipation of the race starting in thirty minutes.

Two bowls of steaming soup sat on the table with spoons and napkins.

"I got myself a Coke," Sarah said. "What do you want to drink?"

"I'll have a Yuengling."

"I saw that in there. My dad loves Yuengling. You know it's made in Pennsylvania, right?"

"Yep. Oldest brewery in America."

Sarah brought the Yuengling to the table and sat beside me, placing her hand in mine. "Shall I say grace?"

We never said grace at the table, but my mom always did it silently. I shrugged, "I guess so."

I watched Sarah bow her head. "Dear Lord, thank you for bringing me the love of my life, the person I've always wanted...."

This was odd to me. Yesterday we were having sinful sex, and today she's praying. Those two things don't go together, sort of hypocritical. I thought she was going to thank God for the soup. I felt a bit uncomfortable, and didn't close my eyes. A piece of her hair dipped into the bowl as she prayed.

"...and thank you for the safe flight home. And thank you for this wonderful meal we are about to partake. In Jesus' name, amen."

When she raised her head the soup hair laid back against her shirt. I thought she would feel it, but apparently she didn't. I didn't tell her about it. I was hungry and didn't want any drama about hair in soup and having to take care of a stain.

We finished the soup with light conversation. She wanted to take a walk. I needed to check something on the computer first.

I logged into the website. "Yes!" I screamed. "Triple Lindy won!"

"What?" Sarah shouted from the kitchen as she washed the dishes.

"Oh, nothing. My team just won."

"Cool."

Fifty grand, just like that. Yes!

I went to the kitchen, grabbed another Yuengling from the fridge and chugged it. "Ready for that walk now?"

"Absolutely!"

We strolled around the property as I explained its history. I avoided the guest house, but she didn't.

"That's a cute little place. Can I see inside of it?"

I didn't mean to snap at her. "No! Absolutely not. Off limits."

"Why?"

I felt a warm redness in my neck. "Jennifer's essence is still there and I don't want to disturb it."

Sarah looked at the ground. "I'm sorry."

I breathed the anger away. It's not her fault. "It's okay. I didn't mean to snap at you like that."

"I understand," she replied, "but I don't want to be your substitute for Jennifer. What you had with her is sacred, and I want to honor that. I'm not Jennifer and will never pretend to be."

"Thanks. No offense, but nobody will ever be Jennifer."

"None taken. And don't apologize for something you couldn't control, Danny. Life is weird and unpredictable. Jennifer will forever be a part of you, and I accept that."

What have I gotten myself into?

We walked to the Quonset hut, just beyond the hanger barn. She was intrigued by its shape. "Never seen one of these funny looking buildings before."

"It's called a Quonset hut. My grandpa used it as a greenhouse, but it's just for storage now.

"Can I look inside?"

"Sure."

I opened the door and a bee flew out at her.

She screamed and swatted, "Oh! Oh! Shut the door!"

"Don't worry, he won't eat much." I laughed. "Still want to see inside?"

"No! I never want to go in there."

I couldn't resist kissing her. "Don't worry. You're safe with me."

She grabbed my crotch and moaned. "Let's go."

She pulled me by the hand to the house. We dashed through the kitchen and living room, kissing, unable to get enough of each other.

"This way, baby," I said, guiding her toward the staircase. We scuttled up the stairs, taking off clothes as we went.

We reached the top, naked, pirouetting in lip-locked unison into the first available bedroom. I pushed her onto the bed and attacked her breasts.

Money ran up the stairs, meowing, wanting attention. He jumped onto the bed and patted Sarah on the forehead. Maybe he thought she was Jennifer.

Sarah stopped kissing me. "Money, get out of here!"

He fled, grumbling.

"Don't be mean to him!" I scorned. "He's all I have left!"

"And what am I?" she asked, agitated.

My cell phone rang in my pants on the staircase. It took precedence over Sarah's question. I darted from the bedroom, picked up my pants and grasped frantically for the phone. "Hello?"

"Hey, man," Joseph said, "nice win."

"Thanks."

"You want the money or do you want to let it ride?"

"Let it ride."

"I don't normally call my clients when they win, but I wanted to do something for you."

"What's that?"

"I'm adding fifty K to your limit. You'll be good for a hundred K now. It's like playing with house money on the fifty K you just won."

"That's cool, but why would you do that out of the blue?"

"First, I know you're good for it. Second, I'm a business man who takes care of his best clients."

I'm sure his intent was to get me to blow the fifty K and bet the rest trying to win it back. I thanked him anyway and hung up.

Sarah was sitting on the side of the bed, staring out the window.

I sat down and put my arm around her. She pushed it off. "I'm beginning to think this was all a big mistake, Danny."

I should have agreed, but I didn't. The sex was too good. "No, baby, this is not a mistake."

She stood up. "Whatever. I'm leaving."

I should have let her go, but I grabbed her wrist, "You can't go. You remind me of Jennifer. You can't leave."

"Remind you of Jennifer? Oh my god!"

"Except for the glasses," I replied, "and that mole on your tit. You're a dead ringer otherwise."

"Fuck you, Danny Dedd!"

She stopped at the top of the stairway and turned around, "I thought we had something great here. I thought you loved me. But all you want is a replacement for Jennifer. I'm not her, Danny! I'm not her!"

I stood up, "What the fuck do you want me to say?"

"Goodbye, Danny."

"Where are you going? You're naked and you have no car."

She scurried down the stairs, "I'll figure it out, asshole!"

Money screeched like someone had stepped on his tail. Sarah screamed and there was a tumbling sound, ending with a big thud.

I ran to the top of the staircase and gazed down at the body lying motionless on the floor. For a reason I could not explain, a calm fell upon me. There was no urgency to ascertain her condition.

Money was meowing beside me. I picked him up, "You okay?" He purred. I stroked his head and put him down.

I looked at Sarah and felt a bizarre sense of satisfaction that I no longer had to deal with a potentially complicated relationship, which might have ended in misery anyway, yet remorseful that the great sex was gone.

I put on my pants and walked slowly down the stairs. I reached down to feel a pulse - slight, but still there.

She landed on my shirt, so I pulled it free and put it on. Her head moved slightly. I heard her struggling to breathe.

She looked different now, lying there naked. The bottoms of her feet were dirty. She also had a large mole on her ass, bigger than the one on her tit. If only I had seen that in Vegas, things might be different. There was a tattoo of a pink ladybug on the small of her back. Cute. Nice detail.

I was annoyed by the dilemma before me. I thought about calling 911, but I didn't want the drama of having to explain what happened, and I would feel obligated to care for her should she be paralyzed.

I bent down, placed both of my hands around her neck and squeezed. She jerked and kicked; apparently she wasn't paralyzed. I pushed hard on her throat until she stopped breathing. No pulse.

I walked to the fridge, opened a Yuengling, and drank it slowly, contemplating what to do with her. I was amazed that I had no guilt, no remorse, and no sense that I had done anything wrong. If that was Money, I'd have rushed him to the hospital.

I knew where I was going to put her. I retrieved a wheel barrel from the barn and placed her tiny body in it. I pushed it to the Quonset hut, slung her over my shoulder and carried her inside. Thankfully, no bees greated me.

I laid her on the dirt floor against the back wall, opened a few bags of potting soil and covered her body. I patted the soil tightly around her until I could no longer see skin, also making sure her nostrils were filled in case she decided to breathe again.

I thought about saying a prayer, but didn't.

I went to the guest house and lie on the bed, smelling the pillow and sheets. I spent the next couple nights there.

CHAPTER 25

❦

Two days passed since Sarah. I was awakened at 9:00 AM by a large truck setting its air brakes in the driveway. I looked out the window and it was United Van Lines. They were delivering Sarah's belongings.

I asked the driver to park beside the small barn. It only took an hour to unload. I made small talk with the driver and his helper, but did not mention whose stuff this was.

The pink Beetle was the last item. I parked it in the barn and gave them both a one-hundred dollar tip.

CHAPTER 26

I sat on the recliner in the living room, feet propped up, drinking a Yuengling. I looked at Money, who was sitting in Bear-Bear's lap, cleaning himself. "Am I crazy, Money? Am I crazy?" He stopped licking, peered at me for a moment, and then returned to cleaning. "I guess I am."

I logged into the gambling website and saw that I now had one hundred thousand dollars to work with. I called Joseph and asked him to increase my line to two hundred thousand. He hesitated and said he'd call me back.

Money jumped onto my lap as I was contemplating which bet to make, so I picked a horse named Money Maker and placed fifty thousand to win.

Good luck charm. Money Maker won the race.

The phone rang and it was Joseph, who explained that he initially was not going to give me a $200,000 line, but since I just won another fifty thousand, he'd do it.

I picked out another horse named Mother's Last Straw and placed a $200,000 bet to win.

Lost by a nose.

I looked at Money, "Well, it's only money." He cocked his head curiously and meowed.

"I didn't mean you, buddy, I meant…never mind."

I called Joseph immediately and said I'd have the $200,000 tomorrow. He said to bring only $100,000, as that's all I owed because of the $100,000 I already won. I set up a time to meet him at Perkins the next day.

I called Derrick to get $100,000 wired to my account, plus another ten thousand for expenses.

"What?" Derrick shouted.

"Don't give me any shit, Derrick. I've got plenty of money."

"What are you doing, Danny? Tell me you aren't into Joseph for a hundred G's."

"That's none of your business. Just wire the fucking money."

"It'll be a few days, Danny."

"Why?"

"This much money takes time to transfer."

"Bullshit! One dollar or a million, it's all the same."

"No, it's not. Just give me a few days."

"I'll give you an hour, Derrick. It better be there. You transferred seven million while I was in your office. Don't fuck with me. Remember Vegas? I'm sure your wife would not be happy if she found out about that."

"You little shit. I thought I could trust you."

"And I you. Wire the money."

I heard Derrick taking a deep breath. "Okay, Danny. A hundred ten G's. It'll be there by the end of the day."

I met Joseph the following morning and paid my debt, all cash.

I decided I would fly to Las Vegas again to find another Jennifer. Perhaps this one wouldn't have a mole on her breast and ass, and maybe Money would like her.

CHAPTER 27

The Jennifer lifted off at noon in route to Las Vegas. Before leaving, I overflowed Money's bowl with food and gave him an extra bowl of water. I then reserved a room at The Paris and called Derrick to ask for the phone number of the call girls.

"Call girls? I thought you didn't want any part of that."

"How about that number?"

"Take me with you and I'll give you the number."

"Nope. This is a solo trip. Give me the number."

"Those girls aren't cheap, Danny."

"Okay, so wire another ten thousand to my account."

"Seriously, don't blow your money on chicks."

"Look who's talking. The number and the money, Derrick."

"725-399-0073. I'll wire the money. Just do me a favor."

"What's that?"

"Don't get herpes."

I laughed, "Yeah, right. I use condoms, unlike you."

I called the number and described what type of girl I wanted and set up a time for that evening.

CHAPTER 28

The Jennifer landed in Vegas and I took a cab to The Paris. I checked into my room and decided to walk the strip.

I avoided The Wynn.

I stopped at a CVS and bought a bag of Wise potato chips and a twelve pack of Bud Light, disappointed that they didn't have Yuengling. I went back to my room and drank most of the beer and ate all of the chips, then fell asleep on the bed.

A loud knock at the door woke me up. I looked through the peep hole, pleased. I opened the door to a short Hispanic vixen, who was scantily dressed. She strutted into the room with a smooth jazzy sway, twirling a silvery handkerchief. White silken stars with dangling tinsel covered her nipples, swaying with each sultry step. She wore panties with sparkly silver sequins.

She circled me silently in her shiny grey pumps, and then took my hand and led me into the bedroom. She tossed the handkerchief in the air and sat down on the bed.

"Like what you see?" She asked.

I shook my head, still waking up, "Uhh…sure. Nice entrance."

"Well, Handsome Jefe, whatta you wanna do?"

"Handsome what?"

"Jefe. Handsome Jefe. It means 'chief' in Spanish. You're a handsome chief."

"You can call me 'Danny'."

"Okay…'Danny'…are we gonna get it on or what?"

"How about a Bud Light first?"

"Sure, baby, whatever you want."

I popped the tops off the last two Bud Lights and handed one to the vixen. She chugged it and tossed the empty bottle onto the floor.

"I guess you mean business," I chuckled.

"You ain't seen no business like me, baby."

"Well," I said, "let me finish this beer and we can do some business."

The vixen removed her pumps, stroked her hair back and reclined onto the bed. "Don't milk that beer, baby, I might lose the feeling."

"I doubt that, but just in case…."

I chugged the beer and placed the empty bottle on the dresser. I knelt at the foot of the bed and inspected her feet. "You have beautiful toes."

"Thank you," she squirmed.

I kissed the top of her feet and began to massage them.

She moaned, grasping the pillows, "Wow." I wasn't sure if she was faking it for the money or not, but I didn't care.

I placed her feet on my shoulders and began to rub her calves.

"You treat all your girls like this, Jefe?"

"Just you, baby, just you."

"I doubt that," she laughed.

I could not ignore the fact that her legs were very similar to Jennifer's – slim, tight and tan.

"Wanna come up here?" she asked.

I stood up, removed all my clothes and crawled up next to her.

"Jesus," she said, "you got the goods, baby."

"Jesus ain't got nothin' to do with it."

"Well," she jested, "somebody sculpted you, Mr. Adonis."

I asked if I could kiss her on the lips.

"Well," she whispered, "normally that's not permitted, but I'll make an exception this time."

I leaned in as she closed her eyes. I bypassed her lips and took a sensual detour across her cheek to her ear. My tongue teased gently on her lobe as my hand rubbed softly on her stomach. Her hips surged as she groaned.

"You're a tricky boy."

My lips worked lightly down to her chest. Her breathing increased.

"Hold on," she insisted, removing her panties.

"By the way," I asked, "how much?"

"What?"

"How much?"

"How much what?"

"How much do you want?"

"I want all of you, baby."

"No, I mean how much money?"

"You sure do know how to kill a moment. It's five hundred for an hour."

"How about three grand to stay the night?"

"You got the cash?"

"Of course."

I pulled out a bundle of Benjamins from the nightstand drawer. "This make you happy?"

"Okay, baby. Get back on me."

I threw the cash on the nightstand and returned to her chest. I removed the silky stars from her nipples with my teeth and spat them onto the floor.

"Oh yeah, baby, let's get rough!" she insisted, pinching both of her nipples as she cupped her breasts.

I licked several times between her breasts and then crouched over her on my hands and knees.

"You gonna titty-fuck me big boy?"

I froze. Her voice sounded just like Jennifer's.

"What's wrong, baby?" she asked.

"You wouldn't believe me if I told you."

"Try me."

I rolled over and stared at the ceiling.

"Well, when you asked me that question just now you sounded like my wife."

"Listen," she said, "I don't want this to get weird. You're paying me to stay the night and I'm willing to do that. Just know one thing – if you ask me to leave now, I'm keeping the three grand."

I took a deep breath. "I don't even know your name. What's your name?"

"You can call me 'Cammie'."

"Cammie. Okay. I want to tell you something."

"Anything, baby, it's your dime."

"My wife recently died in a car accident, pregnant with our first child - a boy - along with my parents. When you asked me about titty-fucking, you sounded just like Jennifer. But she wouldn't ask me that, well, not like that anyway."

"How would she ask you?"

"She never asked. We just kinda knew what was going to happen next. We knew what made each other happy."

"I tell you what," Cammie said, "you just do whatever you want to me and I won't say a word."

"I have a better idea," I said as I got up to put on my clothes.

She squinted her eyes at me. "A better idea? What's better than titty fucking?"

"How about I pay you an additional ten grand to escort me back to Mississippi in my private plane."

"Private plane?"

"Yep."

"Really?"

"Yep."

"No offense, but you don't look like a guy who has a private plane."

"It's a long story. But trust me, I do."

"I'd love to go with you, but let me make sure it's okay with my boss. Do you mind stepping out into the hallway while I make the call?"

"Hallway? Uhh…okay."

I stepped out and she closed the door behind me. A few minutes passed. The door opened and she motioned me inside. She had put on her panties and stars.

"I can go," she said, "but I have to be back here by six o'clock tomorrow evening."

"Not a problem."

"And…" she added, "I need half the money tonight and the other half when you bring me back."

We went to the bedroom and I counted out five thousand onto the bed. "Shall we go now?"

She wadded up the cash and wrapped it in the silk handkerchief. "We need to make a quick pit stop on the way to the airport. I need to deliver this money and grab some clothes."

"No problem."

Our cab arrived at the airport and we boarded The Jennifer.

"You weren't kidding!" she said.

"Nope. Get in. You can be my co-pilot. I'm your star boy tonight."

"I like it," she said.

I pointed The Jennifer due east over Lake Mead and the Grand Canyon. Cammie was in awe of such beauty. She had never seen it from the air.

"I wonder how long it took to make that?" she asked.

"Millions of years. Maybe when I bring you back tomorrow I'll stay a few days and we can drive down to see it up close."

"Really?"

"Sure. I'm always up for an adventure. Do you think your boss will give you some time off?"

"Probably not. I'm at his beckon call twenty-four-seven."

I changed the subject. "Where did you grow up, if you don't mind me asking?"

"Los Angeles."

"Wow, I bet that was exciting."

"If you call being raised by a single mom with five children, having your drunk father found shot dead in a park when you're five, and having to fend off your mother's many boyfriends exciting, then yes, growing up in LA was exciting."

"Oh hell, I'm sorry. That sucks."

"I quit school in tenth grade so I could make some money. I ended up hooked on drugs and working the streets. My boss rescued me and took me to Vegas. Been there ever since."

"Ever think about going back to school?"

"Why? I make over a grand a day doing this, all cash. Uncle Sam doesn't see a penny of it. I make more than most people with college degrees. My boss treats me good. He doesn't beat me. He takes me out to expensive restaurants. I have to give him a little head once in a while, but that's not so bad. He helped me open up a bank account. I've got over half a million in savings."

"It's all yours?"

"Yep."

"Is the boss on the account with you?"

"Yes, but that's just so if something happens to me he gets the money."

"Girl, that's not your money. He could take it anytime he wants."

"He wouldn't do that to me. We've been together a long time. I trust him more than anyone in the world."

"It's none of my business. I just think a beautiful girl like yourself.... never mind."

"Don't worry about me, Danny. I can take care of myself."

"I'm sure you can."

"Hey, you got anything to drink in here?"

"Sure. Grab us a couple cans of Coke from the fridge. It's back there beside the sink."

She returned with the Cokes and buckled in. "Hey, how'd you get so rich?"

"Family money."

"Yeah, so how'd they make all their money?"

"Long story short - farming and mortgages."

"So, it's all yours now?"

"Yep."

"What's it feel like to be filthy rich?"

"I'd give it all away to bring back my family."

"I wouldn't. I mean, I didn't really have a family, so I'd keep the money."

I opened my Coke, chugged half of it and let out a loud burp.

"Weak, Danny, very weak! Watch this!"

Cammie opened her Coke, chugged the entire can and let out two huge belches.

"How are you with baked beans?" I asked, laughing.

"Girls don't fart! You know that."

"Oh yeah, I forgot."

"How long 'til we get to Mississippi?"

"A few hours."

"I saw a couch back there. Mind if I take a nap?"

"That's fine."

CHAPTER 29

As usual, the Jennifer touched down smoothly at the homestead. I unbuckled and walked back to wake up Cammie. I nudged her arm. "Hey, we're home."

She wiped slobber from her cheek with her forearm. "Oh my god, are we here already?" she asked, stretching and yawning.

"Yes. Wake up."

"I didn't even feel us landing. You must be one hell of a pilot."

"Navy."

"Navy?"

"Yep. Fighter pilot."

"No shit! I'd like to hear about that sometime."

"Sometime. Maybe. Let's go. I'm hungry."

Money was sitting on the kitchen table, twitching his tail. I walked in first and gave him some love. "This is my buddy, Money."

Cammie put her hand toward him. "Aww, hey buddy. How are you?" He hissed and jumped off the table.

"Don't worry," I said, "he might warm up to you later."

I pulled a can of Chunky Chicken Corn Chowder from the pantry and showed it to her. "You want some soup?"

"Sure. I love soup."

"Mind grabbing two bowls from that cabinet?"

"Sure. What else can I do?"

"Grab two Yuenglings from the fridge."

"These bottles are green, like Heineken!" she said.

"You just said a dirty word."

"No, I didn't."

"Yes, you did – Heineken. Can't stand it. Gives me a headache."

"How do you pronounce this? Yoo-eng-ling?"

"No. Ying'-ling."

"Sounds Chinese."

"It's German."

"Oh."

I poured the soup into a pan and grabbed one of the beers out of her hand, twisted off the cap and told her to taste it.

"Wow," she said, "that's really good. Better than Bud Light."

"Of course it is. It's from the oldest brewery in the United States. Pottsville, PA."

"PA. Yeah. Isn't that down by Georgia?"

She was obviously geography-challenged. I opened the other beer and took a swig, "Uh, Georgia? No. More like up by Pennsylvania."

"Well, they sure make good beer down there!"

I returned to the soup, amused at her ignorance. "Yes, they sure do."

She walked over to the table and sat down.

"So, Danny, do you have any hobbies?"

"Yuengling. How about you?"

"I like to draw."

"Really?"

"Yeah. I'm no good though."

"What do you like to draw?"

"Anything, really. Animals mostly. I love animals."

I turned off the stovetop eye. "Soup's ready!"

"Awesome," she replied, "I'm so hungry."

I filled the bowls and took them to the table. I walked back to get spoons, napkins and my beer.

"I'm sorry," Cammie said, "let me help you."

"Here," I said, handing her the spoons and napkins, "put these on the table. I'll be right back."

I retrieved a sheet of drawing paper and different sized graphite pencils and laid them on the table. "My mom liked to draw too. Maybe you can draw me a picture after we eat."

"What would you like me to draw?"

"You like animals. Draw me a picture of Money."

""He doesn't like me."

"Don't worry. I'll sit here with him on my lap. He'll sit here as long as I pet him. Let's eat."

I ate quickly, anxious to see how well she could draw. "You want me to go get Money so you can draw him?"

"Sure."

I sat Money on my lap next to Cammie. She reached over to pet him. He sniffed her fingers. No hissing.

"See, I told you. He is warming up."

"He's so sweet," she said.

Her hands scurried with several pencils on the paper. She finished in fifteen minutes and held it up.

"Holy shit!" I said. "You missed your calling. That's amazing!"

She blushed, "No. I'm not really that good."

"Bullshit! It's a perfect depiction of Money sitting on my lap. How did you do that so quickly?"

"I don't know. I just see it on the paper and it feels like I'm just tracing what's already there."

"Please sign it. I'm going to frame it."

She signed it *Camilla Marie Martinez*.

"You have a beautiful name."

"Thank you. I hate it, but thank you."

I sat there stroking Money. "You're a good boy, aren't you? Yeah. You're a good boy."

Money jumped off my lap and went to his food bowl.

"I better fill that up for you, buddy. You ate a lot while I was gone."

Cammie stood up. "Where's the bathroom?"

"Right there." I said, pointing to the door of the half-bath at the corner of the kitchen.

I pulled another Yuengling from the fridge, twisted off the cap and leaned against the island. Money meowed. "Oh, sorry buddy. I forgot."

I sat my beer on the island and grabbed a bag of cat food from the pantry and filled Money's bowl. "Better refresh your water too, little buddy."

Money rubbed against my hand, meowing, as I sat his water bowl next to the food. "You're welcome, little man."

The exhaust fan turned on in the half-bath. She must have been taking a shit.

I returned to my Yuengling at the island. Over the sound of the exhaust fan I heard Cammie passing loud gas.

Jennifer used to do that. But somehow Cammie doing it was a huge turnoff.

I heard her spraying Febreze. I heard the fan stop as she quickly exited the half-bath.

I took a swig of my beer. "Everything work out okay in there?"

She blushed.

I laughed, but she did not appear to be amused. "I'm sorry," I said, "I'm an asshole."

"It's okay," she replied. "Everybody's human. We all do it, right?"

"Of course."

"I'd like to take a shower, if you don't mind," she said.

"Of course. I insist. Come with me."

She followed me upstairs to the hallway bathroom. "Towels are in the closet. Toothpaste is in this drawer with some new tooth brushes. Soap and shampoo are in the shower. Do you want me to bring your duffle bag up here?"

"No, that's okay. Do you have a T-shirt I can wear?"

"Sure." I scurried to my bedroom and grabbed a U2 – Joshua Tree Tour T-shirt from my drawer.

"Thank you," she said. "U2. Cool. Love those guys. Bono is so sexy."

"They're my favorite band. I'm gonna take a shower in the master bedroom across the hall. Just come in there when you're done."

"Okay," she said.

I finished showering, put on a pair of Croft & Barrow boxers, and sat on the end of my parents' bed staring at the floor. This was the very spot where I was made. I wished I wasn't.

Cammie walked in wearing nothing but the U2 T-shirt. Her smooth, tan skin reflected an innocent hue like a virgin ready for sacrifice. She turned off the light and sauntered over to me. She looked and sounded more like Jennifer than a hooker from Vegas. She pushed me gently back onto the bed.

"Would you like a massage?" she asked.

"Absolutely."

She started with my feet, and then slowly worked her way up my legs, stopping momentarily to gently kiss under the bottom edge of my boxers. Shivers ran up my spine. Her hands were soft; her lips gentle and caring.

"You move in mysterious ways, sweetheart," I said.

"Roll over," she insisted.

She caressed my back, shoulders and neck with impeccable precision. If there was Heaven, this was it. I wanted to doze in the comfort.

I felt a sharp sting on my ass where she slapped it.

"Don't you fall asleep, Danny!"

"Ouch! I can't help it. It feels so good."

And then she said something I didn't like.

"Do you mind returning the favor?"

I didn't want to. I was paying her, not the other way around, but I reluctantly agreed.

She lay on her back where I had been laying.

"This feels so warm," she said.

I rubbed my way up her leg. When I reached to top of her thighs I noticed she was not wearing panties. I lifted the T-shirt past her navel. I ran my tongue around it delicately. I avoided her vagina. It was bushy, but smelled nice. There must have been hundreds there before me, which was a turnoff.

She thrust her hips, "Go down on me, Danny!"

I hesitated.

"It's okay, baby," she said. "I don't have any disease."

I opted to insert my thumb. It went inside quite easily.

She shuddered, "Oh god. Yes!"

It sounded authentic, I guess.

I worked my thumb in, out and around.

"Give me your hot tongue, Danny!"

I wanted to throw up in my mouth. I pulled out my thumb, smelled it and sat up. It smelled nice, but I still wasn't putting my tongue in there.

"What's wrong, baby?" she asked.

"Let's dance," I said.

"Dance?"

"Yes. I want to dance."

"Okay, baby. You paid for it. Whatever you want."

I turned on the clock radio on the nightstand. 98.1 FM was playing *Every Rose Has Its Thorn* by Poison.

"Great song!" I shouted. "Let's slow dance!"

"Uh, okay."

She laid her head against my chest.

I closed my eyes, remembering the first dance I had with Jennifer at the Zeta Tau Alpha Spring Fling. I remembered Jennifer's sweet aroma, how she felt in my arms, and how I didn't want that moment to end.

I opened my eyes as Bret finished singing.

Cammie sighed as she kissed my chest.

Enter Sandman by Metallica began to play. Cammie pulled away, "This ain't no slow song, Danny. Change the station."

I forced her close and wrapped my arms firmly around her head, shouting the lyrics, "Sleep with one eye open, gripping your pillow tight!"

"Danny," she shouted, "stop!"

I squeezed tighter, singing louder, "Exit light! Enter night! Take my hand! We're off to never-never land!"

She grabbed fistfuls of my hair. "STOP!"

I kept singing, increasing the pressure on her neck. "Hush little baby, don't say a word. And never mind that noise you heard. It's just the beasts under your bed…in your closet…in your head!"

"You're hurting me!" she shouted.

"Exit light!" I shouted, squeezing as hard as I could.

I felt and heard a loud crack in her neck.

I let go of the limp body and her head slammed against the floor.

I turned off the radio and knelt down beside the body. No pulse. That was good. She was not even close to Jennifer's quality.

I removed her U2 T-shirt and folded it neatly on the bed.

She was light enough to carry straight to the Quonset hut without the aid of the wheel barrel. I laid her beside Sarah and opened a few bags of potting soil. I covered the body, patting the dirt securely into every crevasse, just like Sarah. Perfect. They looked like twins now, only Cammie was a bit shorter.

I stood over them with arms folded. I noticed the tip of Sarah's nose poking through the dirt. "You defiant girl." I threw a handful of dirt on it and patted it firm. "There, sleep tight, baby."

As I stood over them I felt a sudden anger well up inside of me. *How could they betray me like this?* "You both thought you were Jennifer! Look where that got you!"

I took a deep breath. A calmness fell upon me.

I walked into the house, took all the money from Cammie's duffle bag and put the remainder of her belongings in a large garbage can on the back porch.

All this excitement made me hungry. I heated a bowl of Chunky Vegetable Beef soup and enjoyed a Yuengling.

CHAPTER 30

Ten other girls from Vegas completed my collection at the homestead over the next several months. They all lay neatly packed in dirt in the Quonset hut with Sarah and Cammie. They all thought they were Jennifer. They should have known better.

I lay in bed at night wondering if any girl would ever succeed in trying to replace Jennifer. They should probably stop trying, for their own sake. Only Jennifer's love could leave a flawlessly permanent stain on my heart.

The decaying bodies were creating a noticeable stench around the property. I should probably do something about that.

I was proud that I remembered all their names: Sarah, Cammie, Jessica, Uma, Stacie, Tara, Amanda, Diane, Rachelle, Erica, Amy and Mariah.

Between my trips to Vegas, my daily ritual consisted of spending the first few hours at the guest house, soaking up the fading remnants of Jennifer's aroma. I would then walk to the Quonset hut to remind the girls that, had they lived up to Jennifer's quality, they'd still be alive. And so they wouldn't forget, I would call out each of their imperfections - the reasons they had to die.

The next couple hours each day were spent on the gambling website, resulting in my having numerous rendezvous with Joseph in the Perkins parking lot.

CHAPTER 31

It was a sticky Monday morning in June. My effort to pick sure winners the night before were clouded by too many Yuenglings. I amassed a $300,000 debt to Joseph. Those fucking horses might be the death of me.

I called Derrick and told him to wire $300,000 to my account. He said that it was impossible and that he was not going to fund my gambling habit anymore, noting that my father would be highly disappointed.

"I'll sue you, asshole!" I shouted into the phone.

"So, sue me," he replied. "You're going through your money like a fish through water."

"Bullshit! I should have several million left!"

"You don't," he replied.

"Why?"

He hung up.

My next phone call was to Mike Kingston. I explained that Derrick refused to give me money from the trust because he deemed the funds to be for irresponsible purposes.

"What are you spending the money on?" Mike asked.

I took a deep breath. It felt like I was confessing a sin to my father. "I've amassed a large gambling debt...to the tune of $300,000."

There was silence for a couple seconds. "Not the best use of your money, Danny," Mike said calmly, "nonetheless, Derrick has no right to withhold your request."

I cleared my throat. "He said he has a fiduciary responsibility to prevent me from spending it frivolously."

"That's a load of crap," Mike replied. "You can spend it all on Cokes if you want to, or in your case, Yuenglings and Marlboro Lights."

"I gave up smoking, Mike."

"Good. Anyway, nothing in that Trust gives him the right to judge how you spend the money. Why do you think he would say that?"

"I want to believe he's not embezzling my money, Mike."

"I've had my suspicions about him, Danny, but your father sure liked the guy, so I just left it alone. Let me do some digging and I'll call you tomorrow."

"Thanks. And, uh, Mike..."

"Yeah?"

"Thanks for not judging me. You really could have laid into me about the gambling. It's just been so hard losing my family, especially Jennifer. I need to find a way to get my head right."

"Things happen for a reason, Danny. I'm not your judge. Just a friend who cares. I'll call you tomorrow."

"Thanks, Mike."

CHAPTER 32

I woke up Tuesday morning to Money making biscuits on my chest.

"Dude, get off. I'm tired."

Meow.

"Stop! Get off!"

I pushed him off my chest.

He ran to the end of the bed. Meow.

"I know you're hungry. Just give me a sec."

I threw back the covers and waddled into the bathroom, naked, yawning, rubbing my hair. He followed me.

I took a piss sitting down. My mom taught me that so I wouldn't splash it everywhere or pee on the seat.

Money was sitting beside the sink cleaning himself.

"Can I take a shower too?" I asked.

He paused and looked at me, like he understood the question. Meow.

I stood under the hot shower until steam had filled the bathroom. I couldn't stop worrying about paying Joseph.

I turned off the water and grabbed a towel.

Meow.

"Okay, buddy. I'm coming. I'm coming!"

I threw on a pair of worn Levi's and an AC/DC T-shirt.

Meow! Meow!

"Okay! Okay! Let's go!"

I scurried down the stairs with Money close behind. It was a race to see who could get to the kitchen first. As I darted through the living room, he whizzed past me and bounded across the kitchen floor, sliding to a halt next to his food bowl.

Meow.

"You win," I said, catching my breath.

I filled his bowl and sat on the floor petting him while he ate. When he finished, I scooped the litter box and vacuumed the area rug in the living room, the same Persian rug from Sarah's apartment. The green lamps and some of her artwork were also in the house. She was my favorite. They were all downhill after her. If it wasn't for that mole, she might still be here.

I opened the fridge and chugged a Yuengling. I then chopped a white onion, mushrooms, jalapenos and fresh garlic into a sauté pan, and added a splash of balsamic vinegar. When it was browned I added four beaten eggs, salt, pepper and some Slap Ya Mama spice. I toasted two pieces of sourdough bread, made a cup of hot tea, and sat down to enjoy.

My thoughts of Jennifer were interrupted by how I was going to pay Joseph.

My cell phone rang as I was washing dishes. It was Mike Kingston.

"Morning," I said.

"Morning, Danny. I made a few calls last night about Derrick."

"Is it good or bad?"

"Well, all I can say is that your instincts were right. This guy left his previous company under suspicions of embezzlement from a Trust, although it was never proven."

"No shit. That son-of-a-bitch."

"He was given the ultimatum to leave quietly on his own or be fired with criminal charges. He chose to leave."

"So, that's all? He stole someone's money and goes Scott-free? And now he's robbing me blind? How's that fair?"

"They couldn't prove it, Danny. And they didn't want their name tarnished. It was all hush-hush."

"What do we do now?"

"That's not all. Derrick has a serious gambling problem. They suspect he pilfered the Trust to support his habit."

I walked to the fridge for another Yuengling. "So what you're telling me is, I'm screwed."

"Not necessarily. You need to act quickly. Call him and tell him you need to see all the Trust records today. If he refuses, tell him you know why he left his previous employer and your next call will be to your lawyer."

"Thanks, Mike. I'm on it."

I quickly finished my Yuengling, grabbed another from the fridge, and sat down on the recliner in the living room. I dialed Derrick's number.

Voice mail. "Derrick. This is Danny. I need you to call me as soon as you get this."

I downed a few more Yuenglings and went out to the front porch to get some fresh air. The $300,000 was chewing on my soul. I decided to call Joseph and let him know what was happening.

He picked up on the first ring. "You got my money?"

"Look, Joseph, you know I won't screw you. But I just found out our old pal Derrick might be embezzling my money. I need more time."

"I don't give a shit about Derrick or your money problems. I need $300,000 by the end of the day."

"Just give me a couple more days. Please."

"How much can you give me today?"

"I have ten thousand in the bank and another five here at the house."

"Not good enough. I need at least half today and the other half tomorrow."

"Please, just give me until Thursday."

"No."

"What happens if I can't come up with it by tomorrow?"

"You don't want to know," he said, and hung up.

I felt a cold chill fall through me. My cell phone rang as I walked inside. It was that son-of-a-bitch.

"Derrick, you bastard, what the hell…"

"Hey, old buddy! What's up?"

"What the hell are you doing with my money? I need to see all the Trust records TODAY!"

"Not possible, my man. I'm not at the office. Other commitments. I can meet with you tomorrow."

"How can you be so carefree about this? If you don't show me the records today, my next call is to my lawyer. I know why you left your last job."

Silence.

I heard him taking a deep breath. "I will meet you at my office in two hours."

"Two hours, Derrick. Two hours."

I hung up and called Mike. He agreed to meet me at Derrick's office.

CHAPTER 33

I was hungry. I hit a McDonalds drive-thru and got a Big Mac, fries and Diet Coke. So good. So not healthy.

I arrived at Derrick's office in the Poplar Business Plaza thirty minutes early.

As I waited for Mike to arrive, I turned on the radio and listened to a snippet of the Kurt and Rod show.

Kurt was talking about the idiots on the Memphis City Council who approved a two million dollar study of how to make the streets of Memphis cleaner. Rod interjected with comments of what better things could be done with the money, like hiring several temp employees to actually clean the streets, and then there'd be no need for a study of how to do it. There, he just saved the city two million dollars AND solved the litter problem. Kurt interrupted and said 'cleaner' didn't mean literally cleaner, it meant cleaning up the drug problems. Rod digressed. I chuckled. These two characters reminded me of an educated Beavis and Butthead.

Mike pulled in beside the El Camino and I turned off the radio. We walked into the building together.

The receptionist called Derrick and he came out and escorted us to his office. Not a word was spoken until we were in Derrick's office with the door closed.

Derrick started the conversation with a disclaimer that the allegations at the previous company were completely untrue and there was nothing to worry about. He pointed to the Trust records on his desk.

Mike picked up the file. "Do you mind if Danny and I examine these in private?"

"Not at all," Derrick replied, and exited the office.

We spent an hour looking through check registers, account statements and images of canceled checks. The Trust account had been drained to approximately one hundred thousand dollars.

"I'm gonna kill him, Mike. I swear. I'm gonna kill that bastard."

"Hold on, Danny. Don't let your emotions cloud your judgment. We'll get to the bottom of this."

Mike shuffled through several checks. "Look at these, Danny." He handed me a stack of checks made payable to Travertine Corporation.

I quickly added them in my head. "There's over twelve million dollars here! Who the hell is Travertine Corporation?"

"I don't know," Mike replied, "but I'll find out. Tell Derrick to come back in here. But let me do all the talking."

Mike was sitting in Derrick's high back leather chair when Derrick came in.

"Shut the door, Derrick," Mike said, "and sit over there," pointing to the chair in the corner.

I was sitting across the desk from Mike. He turned toward Derrick, who was rubbing his eyebrows nervously.

"We went through the entire file," Mike explained, "and we have a few questions."

"Fire away!" Derrick replied.

"First of all," Mike asked, "who and what is Travertine Corporation?"

Derrick folded his arms. "Travertine is a company that Danny's father invested in a few months before the accident. He told me to move ten million dollars to the company for a thirty percent stake. It's a real estate company in Little Rock."

Mike furrowed his brow. "So, why are you still writing checks to them?"

"I'm not."

"These checks add up to twelve million."

"Oh, that," Derrick replied, "it turned out that ten million was not equal to thirty percent, so I put in two million more."

"Without permission, of course," Mike declared.

"Danny's father said 'thirty percent,' so that's what I did. I was loyal to his desires."

"You still haven't answered my question, Derrick. Who is Travertine?"

"I told you. A real estate company in Little Rock. They own shopping malls and housing developments."

Derrick looked at me. "You know how much your dad loved real estate."

I was about to come out of my chair. Mike held up his hand at me, as if to say 'stay there, don't speak.' He turned his attention back to Derrick.

"Why was the Travertine investment not recorded as an asset in the Trust?"

Derrick closed his eyes, took a deep breath and spoke slowly. "Mr. Dedd told me to get it done as quickly as I could. His sudden passing stopped the whole process of asset registration."

"Bullshit!" I shouted. "My father would have told me or Mike about this. You're a goddamn thief!"

I came out of my chair.

"Danny!" Mike said firmly. "Sit down! I'll handle this."

I was relieved that Mike was so passionate about the situation. I had never seen this side of him. He had my six, as we often said in the Navy. I sat down.

"Okay, Derrick," Mike said, "tell me everything you know about Travertine."

"It's a conglomerate holding of several private real estate developers. There are several partners. I'd be happy to arrange a meeting with them if you like."

"Yes," Mike replied, "call them. Today. Set it up quickly."

Mike stood up and motioned me toward the door.

Derrick tried to shake Mike's hand. The gesture was ignored.

Mike opened the door and pointed at Derrick. "Call me as soon as you have the meeting arranged. Time is of the essence, and I do mean of the essence."

"I understand," Derrick replied.

We showed ourselves out of the building and stood next to the El Camino.

"That's the biggest crock of shit I've ever heard, Mike!"

"Keep your voice down, Danny. I know it's bunk, but we need to beat this guy at his own game. He's in there soiling his pants right now. I'll investigate Travertine as soon as I get back to my office. You sit tight until I call you. It could take a few days."

"I don't have a few days," I mumbled.

Mike patted me on the shoulder. "Go home, son. Sit tight. I've got this."

CHAPTER 34

I drove home recounting my losses: *Jennifer, little Danny, mom, dad, my career, and now my money. What next?*

I needed to get away, despite what Mike said. I couldn't just sit at home. I needed to be in the air, where I felt most at home.

There's a place I loved to go as a kid with my parents. I fired up The Jennifer and set a course for Orange Beach, Alabama, a ninety-minute flight. I could be there by dinner time. Fortunately, I was able to reserve a room at the resort where I had spent several weeks with my parents on vacations: Perdido Beach Resort.

Jennifer joined us at Perdido during the summers of our Junior and Senior years at Ole Miss.

The Jennifer touched down at Jack Edwards National Airport in Gulf Shores, Alabama, only ten miles from Orange Beach.

During my taxi ride to Perdido, fond memories of this area flooded my mind. I visited the Gulf Coast Petting Zoo several times as a child. My father gave me a handful of corn to feed a fawn. As the gentle little baby ate the corn from my hand, its little tail was going a thousand miles an hour. I suddenly found myself laying in the dirt being pummeled by the momma's front hooves. Strangely, I didn't remember any pain from the incident. My father came to the rescue by kicking the momma away from me. We were asked to leave the zoo, which I thought was unfair.

The taxi passed by the Gulf State Park Beach Pavilion, where Jennifer and I once crashed a wedding reception. I played the part of the great Chazz Reinhold from the movie *Wedding Crashers*, and she played the part of a sexy little innocent guest. It had all gone as planned until a drunk man in his fifties started to hit on Jennifer. I wanted to punch him, but Jennifer pulled me out of there.

The lobby at the Perdido Beach Resort smelled clean and inviting, just like I remembered it. The staff was more than hospitable and the room was spotless, with a beach view.

I ordered twelve Yuenglings from room service, to be delivered in a portable cooler. I changed into my swimming trunks and headed for the beach.

I rented a lounge chair at beachside for fifty dollars, which came with soft cushions and a big umbrella. I chose a spot where Jennifer and I once sat for an eternity drinking beer, eating food, laughing, talking, reading, and taking the occasional dip in the gulf to cool off.

I guzzled several Yuenglings, reclined in the chair and gazed out at the gulf, wishing I could go back in time. It was right over there where Jennifer and I embraced in waist-high water and kissed for what seemed like forever. And over there I allowed her to dunk me under water, and then I picked her up and threw her into a crashing wave. We found three perfect sand dollars over there, about the size of fifty cent pieces. We caught small crabs at night right over there and went snorkeling near those rocks.

I closed my eyes and concentrated on the sound of the crashing waves.

I was in a bright room lying naked on a cold, flat rock. Beautiful girls were dancing around me, shouting derogatory comments and poking me with needles and knives. They were faceless, yet familiar. One of them had the body of an angel as she was observing the other girls. She bent down and whispered into my ear, "Would you like to join us?"

I knew this voice, so sweet and soothing. I reached up to stroke her hair. She appeared to be angry. They all dissolved into the light as the flat rock became a lounge chair.

I opened my eyes and took a deep breath as slobber ran down my chin. I wiped it off.

The girl in the neighboring chair asked if I was okay. That familiar voice again. I looked at her. "Oh my god! Baby! You're back!" I reached for her and my hand went through her body.

"Are you okay, sir?"

A lifeguard was standing beside my lounge chair.

I sat up. "Uh. Yeah. I guess I am."

"I just wanted to make sure you were okay," he said, "because you were tossing and turning, shouting the name 'Jennifer' and reaching into the air."

"Yeah. That's my wife."

"Do you need any help, sir? I see your cooler is empty. You might be dehydrated from the alcohol."

"No. I'm okay. Thanks."

I realized I just had a dream within a dream. I picked up the cooler, threw away the empty bottles and started back to my room. I walked through the pool area and heard someone call my name. Turning, I saw an older couple sitting at a table by the bar. The man who called my name stood up. I recognized him as Jim Hugley, a man my parents met years ago at the resort and stayed in touch with all these years.

Jim was a rather large man, a former right tackle for the Cleveland Browns. He used to play catch with me on the beach. He walked over to me and shook my hand and asked if my parents were there. I explained the unfortunate incident and Jim was in disbelief. He handed me a business card and told me to call if I ever needed anything.

"You don't happen to have $300,000 in your wallet do you?" I asked, chuckling.

"Not at the moment," he replied, "but if I did I'd give it to you."

I thought it was strange for him to say that.

"Great to see you, Jim."

"You too, Danny. Take care."

As I arrived in my room I threw Jim's business card beside the TV on the dresser. I took a shower, thinking about where I would like to eat dinner. "Cosmos!" I shouted, as if someone else was in the room. I loved that place.

I put on button-fly Levi's and a T-shirt, anticipating a great meal.

Cosmos was off the beaten path, up route 180 about ten miles. It was famous for Modern Southern eats, with upscale appetizers and posh entrées without big city prices. The décor was fashionably beachy. The taxi driver knew right where it was.

I weaved my way through the waiting crowd on the spacious entry deck to the hostess stand, just inside the front door. There was a forty-five minute wait unless I wanted to sit in the bar area.

I settled into an empty two-seater table against the back wall of the bar.

"Hi!" said a chipper waitress. "My name is Penny and I'll be taking care of you this evening."

She was very attractive, with Jennifer-like qualities. "You'll be taking care of me this evening?"

She smiled. "Yes. Can I start you off with a drink?"

"I'll have a Yuengling."

"Draft or bottle?"

"You have draft? Really?"

"Yep!"

"Oh, hell yes. Bring me the biggest draft you got."

"It's 32 ounces. You okay with that?"

I tapped my index finger on my chin and gazed toward the ceiling. "Uhhh, let me see. Hmmm…yep! I'm okay with that."

"Would you like an appetizer?"

I looked her up and down twice, stopping at her beautiful, dark, Jennifer-like eyes. "Absolutely."

She didn't appear to be insulted by this. She pushed the end of her pen onto her lower lip. "What would you like, sir?"

"Well, let's see. Something fresh and tasty, something that tickles my taste buds yet satisfies my longing."

Her pupils grew large. "Tell me more. I mean, what are you thinking about?"

"Well, you probably don't want to know what I'm thinking about, so just bring me a shrimp cocktail."

She blushed. "Sure thing."

The TV in the corner was showing horse racing, the last thing I wanted to see. I browsed the menu. It all looked good, and nothing looked better than anything else.

"Here's your Yuengling!" Penny announced. "The shrimp should be out shortly."

"Thanks!"

"Are you ready to order?"

"Yes, but nothing here is tickling my fancy. What's your special?"

"Oh my god. I'm so sorry. I should have told you that first."

"No worries."

"Okay. We have a stuffed Red Snapper with garlic mashed potatoes and steamed broccoli. Also, the chef has prepared a…"

I held up my hand. "Say no more. I'll have the snapper."

"It's really good."

"I'm sure it is. I had it here once with my parents."

"You from around here?"

"Nope. Memphis. Well, Tunica, Mississippi, but nobody knows where that is."

"My uncle lives in Memphis. Loves it."

"Really?"

"Yep. He moved up there about ten years ago. He manages the restaurant at the Peabody Hotel."

"Interesting. My wedding reception was at the Peabody."

"I bet that was nice."

"It was amazing. I lost her in a car accident a few months ago."

"Oh my god. I'm so sorry."

"Thank you. Me too."

Penny changed the subject. "Hey, I'll put this order in for you and check on your appetizer."

"Sounds good."

I stared across the room at nothing. My mind wandered. *Penny is so hot. Those perky tits. Her ass. Wow. How in the hell am I going to pay $300,000? Derrick Geyser. That fucking asshole. I should kill that bastard. Or maybe tell his wife about Vegas. I need to just enjoy my time here. Be in the moment. Fuck everything else. Just enjoy the Yuengling.*

My gaze was broken by Penny returning with my shrimp cocktail.

"Here ya go! These are really good. I hope you like them."

"They look great. Are they local?"

"Yep. They were probably swimming off Gulf Shores this morning. We sell a ton of them every day."

"Cool. Thanks."

"My pleasure."

I extended my hand. "By the way, my name is Danny."

"Pleasure to meet you, Danny. You okay on your beer?"

"Go ahead and bring me another one. I'll polish this off in two shakes of a lamb's tail."

"Okay. Be right back."

I dipped a jumbo shrimp into the cocktail sauce, put most of it in my mouth and pinched the tail to fully release it. I closed my eyes and chewed slowly. The flavors burst onto my taste buds. "Mmmm," I muttered. I took another and put it in my mouth before the first one was gone. The horseradish in the cocktail sauce cleared my sinuses. I devoured one after another until all six were gone.

"Pretty good, eh?" Penny said, returning with my beer.

"Oh yeah." I said, still chewing.

"Your snapper should be right out."

I took a swig of beer to wash down the shrimp. "Ahhh! Thank you."

"My pleasure."

I watched her ass as she walked away.

"Zombie! You son of a bitch!" someone shouted, walking towards my table. "How the hell are you?"

"Oh my god! What the fuck are YOU doing here?"

It was Lou Haas, call sign Hulkman, a pilot I flew with during flight school in Pensacola. He stood 5' 8" tall and weighed a buck eighty soaking wet. He was given that call sign one day in the gym as he was struggling to bench press 200 pounds. Someone shouted "Come on Hulkman! Make Lou Ferrigno proud!" And it stuck.

I stood up and gave him a hug. "How the fuck are you, Hulkman?"

"I'm great! How are you?"

"Life's been better."

"I know," he said, "I heard about what happened to your family. I'm so sorry, brother."

"No worries. I'm doing the best I can, given the circumstances. What are you doing here?"

"Brought Sasha here for some down time at the beach."

"How is she?"

"Couldn't be better. Loving the married life!"

"She here?"

"Yeah. She's waiting for me outside. We were just leaving. I left my keys at the table. I looked over and there you were. Holy shit! Great to see you, Danny!"

"Great to see you too, Lou."

"Look, you need to come see us. We're still in Pensacola. Not sure how long though."

"Let's keep in touch," I said.

Lou took out his cell phone. "What's your number? I'll text you."

"901-867-5309"

Lou tinkered with his phone. "Got it. Awesome."

"Take care. And tell Sasha I said hello."

"Will do. Later, man."

"Later."

Penny returned, holding my meal. "Careful, the plate is hot."

"Thanks."

"Old friend?" she asked.

"Yeah. We flew together."

"Flew?"

"Yeah. I was a pilot in the Navy."

"No kidding! How cool."

"Yeah. Long, long story." I looked down at my plate. "Wow, this looks great."

"I hope you like it."

"I'm sure I will. Thanks."

I ate my meal slowly, enjoying every bite. Penny checked in on me every five minutes. Normally, this would annoy me, but I was enjoying her company. She returned again as I finished.

"All done?"

"Yep."

"You having dessert?"

"No. Thank you."

She laid the bill on the table with another piece of paper and walked away.

I picked up the piece of paper. She had written her phone number and address on it with a message: Dessert is on me. I get off in 30 minutes. Meet me.

I threw down two hundred dollars, took out my cell phone and called a taxi.

CHAPTER 35

❦

I was sitting on the front steps of Penny's apartment as headlights pulled into the parking space directly in front of me. Two females got out.

"Been here long?" Penny asked.

"Long enough."

"Sorry. I had to pick up Chloe."

Chloe was a petite blond with a pixie hairdo and bouncy step. She strutted up to me and extended her hand. "Nice to meet you, Danny."

"Nice to meet you too."

She looked at Penny. "Damn, girl, he's hotter than I imagined."

Penny chuckled, "Told ya!"

Chloe said she worked at the Sea-N-Sudds restaurant. She was from Pigeon Forge, Tennessee and left home after high school. Her parents were wealthy and she decided to explore the world before settling on anything serious, like college or marriage.

They escorted me into the apartment. I noticed it was unkempt, with dirty dishes piled in the sink and carpet that was in serious need of vacuuming. I could smell the dirty litter box in the corner of the dining area. I wanted to gag.

"Don't mind the mess," Penny announced. "We barely have time to clean, except on weekends."

I smiled, "Not a problem. Looks like you clean it once a month whether it needs it or not."

"Funny," Penny said, "my dad said the same thing when he was here."

A Siamese cat walked out of the bedroom.

"Bootsy!" Penny yelled. "Come here baby girl!"

Bootsy scampered into Penny's waiting arms. She loved on Bootsy, kissing her head while scratching under her chin.

"Do you like cats, Danny?" Penny asked.

"My best friend is a cat. His name is Money."

"Really? What kind is he?"

"A Tuxedo."

Chloe laughed, "Like Sylvester the cartoon!"

"Yes," I replied.

"Well," Penny said, handing Bootsy to me, "meet Bootsy. She's MY best friend."

"Hey!" Chloe said. "What am I?"

"No offense," Penny answered, "but you know how much I love my Bootsy."

"Interesting," I said as I cuddled Bootsy, "my dad had a cat named Boots when he was a kid."

"Must be fate," replied Penny.

"I love a man who loves pussy," Chloe said.

I laughed, "Well, then, I guess I'm your man."

Penny looked at me, "You ever had two pussies at once?"

My crotch started to tingle. "No. But I'm not opposed to having two. I'm sure it's more than twice the work to keep them happy."

"Not if you let them do all the work," Chloe said.

I smiled, "I like to be in control."

"You should try it," Chloe insisted.

"I wouldn't mind trying, but it would be hard for me to give up the control."

"Not if you had the right pussies," Penny said.

Penny looked at me and winked, "Wanna try?"

"I'm not sure."

"Not sure?" Chloe asked.

"Yeah," I replied, "dirty litter box, dirty pussy."

"Don't worry," Penny said, "we clean our litter boxes daily."

"Good enough for me," I chuckled.

Chloe grabbed Penny and me by the hands and led us into the bedroom.

"This is my room," Chloe said, turning on the light.

The bed was unmade. Clothes were strewn on the floor. A thick coat of dust covered the dresser and end tables. She lit a candle and turn off the light. "There," she said, "now the mess is gone."

"I'll pretend it's clean," I said.

Chloe stripped naked as if her clothes were on fire. She launched herself onto the bed like a little girl who was excited that her daddy was going to read a bedtime story.

Penny put in a U2 CD - *The Joshua Tree* - and slowly removed her clothes to *Still Haven't Found What I'm Looking For*. She lay beside Chloe. They giggled and played with each other.

I was enjoying watching this lesbian porn. Chloe and Penny explored each other as if I was not there.

I removed my clothes and stood at the foot of the bed, pleasing myself.

The girls noticed me and sat up to watch.

"Oh my god," Chloe whispered, "it's perfect."

"He's got great command of it," Penny said.

Penny stood on her knees at the foot of the bed and started to work her tongue around my nipples. Chloe scurried for my prize like a starving lioness. Penny's tongue worked its way down my abs to join Chloe in a tandem effort.

I closed my eyes and tilted my head back. My thoughts wandered through the Quonset hut girls who had similar talents. I imagined each one and their particular skills.

These two girls in the moment were covering all the bases. They were experienced enough to know when to stop, avoiding discharge. It was like revving up a muscle car, slamming it into gear and letting off the gas half way to the finish line. They were coasting me to the checkered flag.

All I wanted to do was drive it home. They pulled me onto the bed, turning me face up. One nipple for each of their tongues. They worked their way up to my neck while their hands took turns keeping me at attention.

My hands found their way to every part of their bodies, with my middle fingers coming to a slippery rest inside of them.

Chloe broke away and climbed on top of me. Penny's tongue continued to explore, finding a ticklish spot here and there.

I grabbed Penny's hair and brought her to my mouth, and then my hands investigated all that they could reach.

Chloe soon squealed with pleasure. I felt her vagina tightening, pulsing as her pelvis shuddered. She invited Penny to take her place.

Penny rode me with a subdued nature, like enjoying a sunset at the beach. She was very deliberate in her pacing. This turned me on more than Chloe's animalistic romp.

I announced that I was nearing the edge. Penny begged me to hold on a little longer, unwilling to give up what she had.

I did my best to think of something non-sexual to hold back the pinnacle. To my surprise, Penny soon cried out that she was there, so I exploded inside of her.

Soon we all lay together, caressing in a triumvirate glow until I announced that I didn't mean to eat and run, but I had to get up early to meet friends at the airport. I lied. This was fun, but thoughts of owing $300,000 to Joseph crept in. I was glad that this was not on my mind while Penny was on top of me. I would have probably gone limp.

"Don't go!" Penny begged.

"Stay for a few more songs," Chloe said.

With Or Without You was playing and Penny asked me to lay there until it was over. I conceded while they embraced me with eyes closed.

The song ended. We got dressed and went to the stinky kitchen.

Penny opened the fridge. "Care for a Bud Light? I don't have any Yuengling."

"That's cool," I said. I drank it as fast as I could and made known my intentions to leave.

They latched onto me and said it was one of the best nights of their lives. They took turns kissing and hugging me goodbye.

"When will we see you again?" Chloe asked.

I opened the door. "It might be a while. I have a lot of business to tend to at home. You both are amazing. Thank you for an incredible evening."

I fought the urge to take them both to the homestead, just for fun, but that would not be the right thing to do. They didn't display any notion of wanting to replace Jennifer. Besides, the debt to Joseph trumped adding two more beauties to the Quonset hut.

CHAPTER 36

⁘

A cab took me back to the resort. I had thoughts of ending Derrick's life and how I could accomplish that. I also imagined walking up to Joseph in the Perkins parking lot and putting a bullet through his head. Neither of these seemed to be a smart option. I was stuck. I had to face the fact that I had to pay, but didn't know how.

I walked into the lobby at Perdido, ready to retire for the evening. That familiar voice stopped me again.

"Great to see you again, Danny!"

"Hey, Jim. Nice to see you too."

"Listen, Danny, I was thinking about what you said to me earlier today."

I cocked my head in curiosity, furling my eyebrows.

Jim put his hand on my shoulder. "I know you were kidding about the $300,000. But if you need any financial help, I can be of assistance."

"I appreciate that, Jim. Actually, I do need some help, but it's nothing I can't handle myself."

"I'm sure," he said, "but your father helped me when I was down and out. Bad investments, ya know. He never expected me to pay him back. But I promised myself I would someday. And now that he's gone, I won't get to do that."

Jim removed a checkbook from his back pocket. "Come over here," he said.

We sat at a table as he wrote a check to me for $100,000. "This is the same amount your dad gave to me, and now I'm giving it back."

"I can't accept this, Jim."

"Make an old man happy and take it. Seriously. I can afford it, Danny. I really need you to take this."

I reluctantly took the check, folded it once and put it in my front jeans pocket. "I'm taking this for my dad, Jim, and to help you clear you conscience. I really don't need this."

"Thank you, Danny. I'm sorry that your dad is gone. I loved that guy."

"Me too," I said as I stood up to leave. "Me too."

Jim shook my hand and wished me well.

CHAPTER 37

I woke up Wednesday morning exhausted from worry. I took a slow, hot shower, dried off and laid the wet towel neatly on the bathtub edge. I looked at myself in the mirror. *I can do this.*

I walked to the bed where I had previously laid out my clothes. I put on my boxers, jeans, a U2 T-shirt, and pulled on my white Nike socks and Nike sneakers. I picked up the TV remote from the dresser, noticing Jim Hugley's business card.

A shock wave ran through my body as I read the card: Jim Hugley, President, Travertine Corporation.

Holy shit. You've got to be kidding me!

I grabbed a bagel from the free continental breakfast, took a taxi to Jack Edwards National, and flew The Jennifer back to the homestead.

CHAPTER 38

Money greeted me at the front door with a meow. I picked him up and loved on him for a minute. "Hey, buddy! How ya doing? Miss me?"

I filled his bowls with food and water, and then scooped the litter. I should have taken Bootsy. She'd love it here. At least she'd have clean litter.

I went to the fridge for a Yuengling, popped off the cap and chugged it. "Ahhhh!"

My cell phone rang as I threw the bottle into the garbage can. It was Mike Kingston.

"Mike, you're not going to believe this."

"Danny, I've got some news…believe what?"

"My father's friend, Jim Hugley, is the president of Travertine Corporation."

"Yes. I know."

"You know?"

"Travertine is a mob operation. Derrick wasn't wrong when he said they were into real estate, he just didn't tell us the whole story. They buy bad debt from illegal gambling operations. They've built a rather large portfolio of hard assets from extorting the debtors – houses, shopping malls, restaurants, machinery, you name it. Jim is the front man for these 'legitimate' businesses."

"So, why was my dad sending them so much money?"

"I don't think your dad knew anything about it. I think Derrick was into them for millions and was paying his way out with the Trust money."

"My dad gave Jim a hundred grand once and Jim never paid him back. But he gave me the money when I saw him at Perdido Beach yesterday. He said he had been in trouble and my dad helped him out of a jam."

"First of all, why did you go to Perdido Beach when I told you to stay home? Never mind. What did you do with the money?"

"It's in my pocket. He wrote me a check."

"That's dirty money, Danny. Don't cash that check. You don't want any links to this when it goes down."

"Too late."

"What?"

"I hate to tell you this, but I'm into a bookie for $300,000."

"Jesus, Danny. You don't have that kind of money."

"I thought I had millions."

"Let's take this one step at a time. You need to find a way to pay that bookie. I'll work the legal end against Derrick."

"Derrick is broke, Mike."

"I'm not talking about getting the money back. It's gone. But we might be able to put Derrick away for a long, long time if we can prove embezzlement."

"You know I can't pay you, Mike."

"Don't worry about that. Just deal with that bookie, son."

CHAPTER 39

⚬⊗⚬

I grabbed another Yuengling from the fridge and went to the living room to relax on the recliner. I tapped nervously on my cell phone as I swigged the beer. Mike's words resonated over and over in my mind – *Just deal with that bookie, son.*

Money jumped onto my lap. His cold nose touched my forearm. I stroked his head.

"What would you do in this situation, Money?"

Meow.

"Really?"

Meow.

"Yeah. Me too."

I dialed Joseph's number. He picked up on the first ring.

"Too late, kid."

"What?"

"Too late."

"Too late for what?"

"I sold your debt."

"You didn't even give me a chance. I have $100,000 today and I can get you the rest next week."

"Can't do anything about that now. You'll have to deal with them."

"Them who?"

"Don't worry about it."

"What's their number? I want to call them."

"You don't call them. They call you. Or they pay you a visit."

"Fuck! You mother fucker!"

Joseph hung up.

I pounded my fist on the arm of the recliner. Money screeched and jumped off my lap, clawing into my thigh with his back feet.

"Ouch! What the fuck!"

He ran to the kitchen and hid under the table.

"Sorry buddy! Daddy's just upset. Not your fault."

Meow.

I reclined, contemplating all my options. *Take the hundred grand and fly away and start a new life. No. Sell the homestead or The Jennifer. No. Kill Derrick. Maybe. Well, no. Ask Mike for the money. No. Call Jim Hugley. Yes. Maybe he can help.*

I removed Jim's business card from my wallet and dialed the number.

"Jim Hugley," he answered.

"Hi, Jim, it's Danny Dedd."

"Hey, Danny! It was great to see you. How ya doin'?"

"I could be better."

"How's that?"

"I need some advice."

"Hold on, Danny."

I heard a garbled conversation that went on for a couple minutes.

"Sorry about that, Danny. Had to let my wife know I was going outside to take this call. She got a little temperamental. Women, right? Now, tell me what's going on."

"I'm just gonna level with you, Jim. I know what Travertine does and I think they are coming after me."

"So, you weren't joking when you said you needed $300,000."

"No. Not a joke. I need help, Jim. I told my bookie I had $100,000 today and can have the rest next week. He said he sold the debt. I'm assuming it was to Travertine."

"Who's the bookie?"

"Joseph somebody. From Memphis."

"Yep. He's a real asshole. Most bookies would have taken your offer. He's quick to sell out. Travertine buys from him a lot, so, yes, it's probably Travertine."

"Can you talk to your people and ask them to take my offer?"

"Look, Danny, I'm really sorry about your situation, I really am. But there's nothing I can do about it. I run the real estate area, not the leg breaking area. My advice to you is to come up with the money or some kind of asset that is worth twice what you owe. These guys don't mess around."

"How the hell did you get involved with Travertine?"

"Long story. Let's just say I owed them a lot of money at the same time they needed a legitimate face, like a former NFL player, to run their real estate portfolio. They forgave my debt for a ten year commitment. I've been with them for fifteen years now. They pay me a lot of money to keep my mouth shut. I've told you too much already."

"That money my dad gave you. Was that for…."

"Yes. Gambling debt. Listen, Danny, I want to help you, but I can't. You understand, I'm sure."

"Sorry to bother you," I said as I hung up.

I took a deep breath. *I could offer them The Jennifer or the homestead. Hell no. I'm not paying a dollar for a nickel's worth. Fuck that. I can get out of this. I'm smart. Think. Just think.*

I dialed Derrick's number. He answered and went straight into business.

"Tell Mike I'm still trying to get that meeting set up with the Travertine partners."

"Oh, really?" I replied, tempted to tell him I knew it was all a lie. "How many partners have you called?"

"Uhh…four."

"Which ones?"

"Don't worry about that. Just tell Mike I'm still working on it."

"You can tell him yourself. I didn't call about that."

"Then why did you call?"

"I need you to deposit the remaining $100,000 from the Trust into my bank account. Today."

"Not a problem," he replied, and hung up.

I thought about the $100,000 check from Jim. I decided to deposit it in the bank, against Mike's wishes.

I walked to the kitchen. Money was still lying under the table.

"Wanna go for a ride, buddy?"

Meow.

I drank another Yuengling, picked up Money and fired up the El Camino. He found a comfy spot on my lap before we were out of the driveway.

CHAPTER 40

It felt like a pre-heated oven in the El Camino. I wound the window down to get some relief. I turned on the radio and soon realized I had to go to the bathroom. Shouldn't have chugged that last beer. I pulled into a gas station, turned off the El Camino and rushed into the store.

I finished my business in the filthy bathroom, and then purchased a single large bottle of Busch beer for the road – there were no large bottles of Yuengling.

When I returned to the El Camino I jumped in and started the engine. A terrifying thought struck me as I was about to put it in reverse – *where's Money?*

Shock waves darted through my body.

Oh my god he must have jumped out the window. I'm such an idiot!

I turned off the El Camino and looked underneath it. Not there. Not in the bed either. I lifted the hood. Not there.

I walked around the parking lot asking people if they recently saw a black and white cat. No luck.

I went back into the store and questioned customers and employees. No luck.

I walked around the building, shouting, "Money! Money!"

I looked in the garbage dumpster. Not there either. "Dammit, Money. Come on, man."

Tears welled up in my eyes. I had lost everything I ever loved, and now Money. I contemplated calling the police and then realized how silly that might sound. I stood beside the El Camino, not sure what to do.

Maybe he ran down the road. Or maybe someone took him.

I got back in the El Camino, started it, turned off the radio and drove slowly out of the parking lot onto Highway 61.

Meow.

Was that a meow?

Meow.

Oh my god, it's coming from under the seat!

I stopped on the side of the highway.

Meow.

I bent over and looked under the passenger seat. "Money! Oh my god, it's you!"

I pulled him from his hiding place and sat there petting him for a few minutes. "I thought I lost you, man. Don't ever do that to me again."

He licked my hand. Meow.

Relieved, I drove to the bank to deposit Jim's check. I pulled into the drive-thru and asked the teller if there was another large deposit into my account today.

"No, sir," she said.

Derrick had not made the deposit. Bastard.

When the teller saw Money she sent out a cat treat with the deposit slip. I thanked her and started back to the homestead while drinking the large Busch beer and considering my options. Money ate the treat and then climbed onto the back of my neck for the ride home. The vibration of his purring comforted me. I couldn't stand the thought of losing him.

I called Derrick to ask him about the deposit. Voice mail. I told him I went to the bank and the deposit was not there yet and it needs to be done today. No excuses.

I took Money home, turned the El Camino around and pointed it toward Memphis. I was going to see Derrick.

CHAPTER 41

I had just crossed over the state line into Tennessee when my phone rang. It was Mike.

"Danny," he said in a serious tone.

"Hi, Mike."

"I've been worrying about you. Did you deal with that bookie?"

"Sort of."

"What do you mean 'sort of'?"

"That bastard already sold my debt."

"Sold it?"

"Yes. Sold it. To Travertine."

"Call Jim Hugley," he insisted. "Maybe he can help you."

"I did."

"And?"

"He can't. Long story. He just can't."

"You need to watch your back, Danny. This will probably get worse before it gets better."

"When are you going to file charges against Derrick?"

"Probably next week. But there's something else I need to talk to you about."

"What's that?"

"The Tunica County Sheriff called me."

I felt my voice cracking. "Why?"

"He wanted to know where to find you. He said he stopped by the house a few times but you weren't there."

"Did he tell you what he wanted?"

"He said there were several girls missing from Las Vegas and you were a suspect."

I swallowed hard. A numbness fell over me. "What? Are you serious?"

"Danny, what's going on?"

"Nothing. I swear. I flew out to Vegas a few times to gamble. Derrick went with me once. That's when I suspected he was stealing my money."

"The money doesn't matter now, Danny. The Sheriff told me he received a call from the Las Vegas police. It seems your plane had been logged at the airport on the same days each girl went missing."

"I had fun with a few girls there, but I didn't kidnap anyone. This is all a coincidence. I assure you."

"I'm sure it is. Nonetheless, you need to call the Sheriff to get this cleared up."

"I will. Thanks."

My hands were shaking as I ended the call. I pounded on the steering wheel. "Fuck! Fuck! Fuck!"

I turned up the radio to drown my thoughts. White Stripes' *Seven Nation Army* was pounding from the speakers. I could barely keep the El Camino straight as I screeched into the parking lot at Poplar Business Plaza.

I drove around the busy plaza looking for a parking spot, eventually finding a tight one in the back row, shaded by an overgrown Crape Myrtle with pink and white blooms. I sat there with my head against the steering wheel. After five minutes the heat was unbearable. Sweat dripped from the end of my nose as I was trying to talk myself out of walking into Derrick's office and beating the shit out of him.

I squeezed out of the El Camino, careful not to bang my door into the mini-van next to me. I flicked the door shut with my index and middle fingers while shuffling sideways between the two vehicles, arms in the air.

I was startled by a man leaning against the back of the mini-van. "Got a dollar you can spare, sir?"

I instinctively retreated a few steps. "Sorry, man, no cash on me."

"Well, God bless you anyway, sir."

I turned to walk away as a white, six-wheeled cargo van sped down the row. The name *Lone Eagle Bakery* was faded on the side of it, beneath someone's poor attempt to spray paint over it. An icon of a bald eagle clenching a baguette was still visible on the driver's door.

I sprung back, nearly clipped by the front bumper. I was unable to resist the urge to flip the driver a double bird.

He slammed on his brakes and the tires smoked to a screeching halt.

I froze.

The driver, a broad-shouldered, burly man, jumped out with a wicked purpose, his eyes burning into me with each rushing stride. The passenger door slammed and I heard committed footsteps on the other side of the truck.

"Uh oh!" shouted the homeless man.

My self-defense training in the Navy taught me to stand my ground in the face of an imminent threat. I prepared myself for a brawl.

The burly man brandished a .40 caliber Glock pistol.

My hands went up, palms-forward at eye level.

He stretched to hold the barrel against my forehead, "You wanna flip me off again, mother fucker?"

I felt the skin on my forehead tighten into the point of the cold barrel.

"Sorry, sir," I said, hoping to diffuse the situation.

"Ain't no 'sir' about it, asshole, get down on your...."

I reacted without conscious thought. My left hand swept across the barrel, grabbing it tightly as my right palm thrusted into the burly man's wrist, breaking his grip. In less than a second I now held the Glock, pointing it at him. I snapped a punch square to his jaw, stunning him for a moment.

I heard footsteps bearing down on me from behind. I snapped around and landed a dazing round-house kick to the head. The man fell and lost grip on the aluminum bat that he was about to use on me. It pinged against the pavement and rolled against the rear tire of the van.

I heard a yell and, turning, side-stepped a poorly attempted punch from the dizzy burly man. I pointed the Glock at him. "Move over there next to your buddy."

"Hey you," I said to the homeless man, "pick up that bat and put it in my car."

"Sure thing, boss," he replied.

I was sure these were Travertine guys. Made no sense that it could be anyone else. I motioned them to the front of the van with the Glock. "Get the hell out of here before I shove this Glock up your asses!"

The burly man opened the driver-side door. "You have no idea who you just fucked with."

"Neither do you. Now get the fuck out of here!"

I heard feet shuffling behind me. I turned my head to see who it was. The homeless man was swinging the aluminum bat toward my head.

I was unable to block it.

CHAPTER 42

❦

No light penetrated the blindfold that was tightly secured around my eyes. The air was damp and chilly. A stale odor reminded me of the old potato bin in my parents' basement, where I used to hide from invisible monsters.

My head was throbbing with pain above my left ear. I was handcuffed to the sides of what felt like a heavy, cold steel chair, and my wrists hurt.

I heard the familiar click of a Zippo lighter; then someone inhaled and snapped the lid shut. Cigarette smoke filled my nostrils.

Fluid - blood I supposed – was trickling into my left ear. I was unable to reach it with my shoulder to rub away the tortuous tickle. I tried to shake it away, but the pain was unbearable. I had a concussion once, at fifteen, when I fell onto the barn floor from the top of a cotton picker. This felt much the same. I was sleepy and wanted to throw up.

Someone smacked me with their hand on my injury. "Ouch, you mother fucker!" I shouted.

I heard the Zippo open again, and the overwhelming stench of lighter fluid filled my nostrils. He must have been holding the Zippo under my nose, unlit. The instant nausea I felt reminded me of the jet exhaust poisoning I experienced during pilot training. I turned my head to the side and vomited.

The person laughed. It was a man.

He removed my blindfold, still laughing as he took a deep drag from the cigarette and casually blew it upward. The smoke huddled around the single fluorescent bulb glowing dimly above my head.

"Where am I?" I asked.

The man took another drag. "Nowhere," he said, blowing out smoke. I recognized his voice. The burly man.

"Who are you?" I asked.

He took another long drag and blew it in my face. "Nobody."

I coughed. "Asshole."

He slapped my wound again.

The pain jolted through me. "Goddamn it, knock it off!"

He snorted, hocked up a snot ball and spat it into my hair.

I struggled in the chair. My wrists felt raw and swollen. I almost tipped over, save the burly man intervening to bring me upright.

I tried to bite his arm and he slapped my head again.

"If you're going to kill me, just do it!"

"Soon enough," he said, exiting the room, "soon enough…asshole."

CHAPTER 43

I heard muffled voices outside the door. I was able to comprehend parts of the conversation. They spoke about inflicting pain. Someone kept saying my name, and I heard someone say 'Joseph'.

My eyes were heavy and I caught myself falling asleep several times. I gave up trying to stay awake.

I was sitting in a restaurant with my parents and their friends, Bill and Lisa Bugg, a couple who made their wealth from owning several car dealerships. They had since retired and lived in a mansion outside of Senatobia, Mississippi. Bill was mid-sized, had long hair with a Grateful Dead-like, free-spirit appearance. Lisa, a tiny blonde, was somewhat reserved and had a sharp business mind. She wore black rimmed glasses, which Bill referred to as her sex goggles.

I looked around the restaurant as it turned into a disco club. I was slow dancing with Jennifer. We stared into each other's eyes as Steve Perry was crooning *Foolish Heart*. Half way through the dance Jennifer hit me over the head with an empty beer bottle.

I jerked awake to find the burly man standing beside me, fist clenched.

Through the dim light I saw three other men against the wall, wearing black pants and white shirts; their handguns were resting in shoulder holsters.

"Are you guys from Travertine?" I asked.

The burly man punched my jaw. "Don't speak unless you are spoken to."

Blood trickled from my mouth. I spat out a tooth, which bounced across the floor.

The burly man chuckled. "I'd like to see that again."

He drew back his fist.

"No!" said one of the men, who appeared to be in his late forties with a shaven head and goatee, and had the build of a former Mr. Universe. He placed a chair backwards in front of me and sat down. He folded his arms and stared into my eyes. I looked at him, and then dropped my gaze to the floor. He reached over and lifted my chin.

"Do you know who I am?" he asked.

I nodded 'no'.

"Well, please allow me to introduce myself. My name is Franco."

My blood and saliva dripped onto his hand.

He let go of my chin and wiped his hand on my shirt. "And I'm also your worst fucking nightmare if you don't pay $300,000. Cash. Today."

I spat to the side and spoke in contempt through the pain. "Like I told Joseph, I can have $100,000 today and the rest next week."

The burly man slapped my ear.

Franco held up his index finger and smiled. "No need for that."

"Sorry," said the burly man, backing away.

Franco stared at me for a moment. "If you think you're in pain now, you should see what's in store for you if you don't pay everything today."

I spit in his face. "Go to hell!"

He cleaned himself with his shirt sleeve. "Look what you've done, Danny. My nice white shirt is stained now."

He stood up and pulled away his chair. He looked at the burly man. "You know what to do."

The blindfold was placed around my eyes again. Someone cut off my shirt. They tied me to the chair with nylon rope around my chest and thighs. The rope dug into my sternum, and the blood supply was slowing in my lower legs. The more I squirmed, the more painful it became.

A loud, intimidating sound filled the room. I knew what it was. I was about to get hit with a stun gun.

The Navy did this to pilots as part of torture training. Only then I wasn't bound and handcuffed to a steel chair. I prepared myself for what was next. I clenched my jaw, flexed all my muscles, and took deep, rapid breaths.

"This is going to hurt you a lot more than it hurts me," Franco mused. "Do it."

The burly man pressed the stun gun onto my chest and compressed the trigger. Over three million volts ran through my body. Every muscle pulsated violently. He held it there for an eternity before Franco yelled for him to stop.

I was coherent but couldn't control my limp body, slumping motionless in the chair. Lactic acid burned through my muscles. My wrists were numb from the handcuffs, and my chest was raw beneath the rope.

Franco whispered into my ear. "Want more?"

I was able to sit up through the exhaustion. "No. No more," I said, gasping for air.

"Well," said Franco, "the only thing that will make it stop is $300,000. Today."

I didn't want any more pain, but I wasn't going to promise anything I couldn't deliver. I struggled to catch my breath. "$100,000 today…$200,000 in three days. Please. I can do that. I promise."

"Want me to hit him again, boss?" said the burly man.

"No." Franco replied. "Here's what we are going to do, Danny. Since I'm a merciful fellow and I kinda like you, you are going to give me $200,000 tomorrow. And you will get me $100,000 on Friday. If you don't have the $200,000 tomorrow, I will double your debt and increase the pain to the point you'll want to be dead. Am I clear?"

I took a deep breath. "Crystal. I promise."

Franco held a rag over my mouth. The last thing I heard was "Nighty night."

CHAPTER 44

∞

I woke up shirtless, sitting in the El Camino at Poplar Business Plaza. I wasn't sure how long I was out, but it was still daylight. I felt like I was severely hungover and dehydrated. Despite the shade from the Crape Myrtle, the inside of the El Camino felt like an oven. I rubbed my jaw as my tongue examined the missing tooth hole. My wrists were ringed with dried blood, stiff and sore. All of my muscles ached, and the lump above my ear was very tender to the touch.

I started the El Camino and drove to the closest CVS pharmacy to find a shirt and medicine.

An employee, a fifty-something black lady stocking a shelf near the door, told me I wasn't allowed in there without a shirt. I told her I had a rough day and really needed a T-shirt.

She apparently saw my abrasions. "Oh my god, are you okay, darlin'?"

"Yes, ma'am. Like I said, rough day."

She escorted me to a small selection of shirts, and the only one that fit me was pink with *'Girls Rule'* on the front of it.

"Considering the circumstances, it looks good on you," she said. "You want something for your boo-boos?"

"No, thanks. Just the shirt."

I paid with some cash from my front pocket and thanked her for being so kind.

I realized I was hungry, so I drove to the Perkins restaurant where I had met Joseph many times. A Memphis police car followed me partway. I kept an eye on him in the mirror. I wondered if he was running my plate.

He turned onto Highland and I sighed with relief.

The smell of delicious Perkins food overwhelmed my senses when I walked in, but I went straight to the bathroom to look at myself. My hair was clumped with blood above my ear. I wiped it the best I could without making it bleed. I washed my face and did whatever I could with my hair. The cold water on my face felt refreshing.

I requested a booth next to the windows facing the parking lot. I wanted to keep an eye on the El Camino. Someone laughed as I passed their table. Must have been my shirt.

The waitress was a nice looking Hispanic girl. "You okay?" she asked in the softest voice. Reminded me a little of Jennifer.

"Yeah, I'm alright. Bad day."

"We all have those sometimes. What can I get you?"

"I'll have a cheeseburger, fries and a large Coke."

I finished the meal like a starving dog, paid with a credit card and left the pretty waitress a twenty dollar tip.

I drove back to the Poplar Business Plaza and walked up to Derrick's office window. He was on the phone with his feet propped on the desk. I tapped on the window. He turned around, surprised. I pointed toward the front door. He hung up and came out to meet me in the lobby.

There was no conversation as we walked to his office, yet it was not awkward for me. I rushed ahead of him in the hallway. I plopped into his high-back leather chair and he begrudgingly took a seat across the desk.

I propped my feet on the desk and folded my arms. I hoped the glare in my eyes looked serious. "Why haven't you deposited the hundred grand?"

"I've been extremely busy, Danny, and I don't have time for this bullshit. You are sucking the Trust dry."

I sat up and pounded my fist on the desk. "Just put the last hundred thousand in my account. Now!"

He looked at me and chuckled. "Where did you get that shirt? It's hard to be serious staring at *Girls Rule*."

"YOU are the reason I'm wearing this shirt, you asshole. You referred me to Joseph!"

"You lose some money?"

"The price just went up. Put $200,000 in my account."

"You can't get blood from a turnip, Danny. I'll put in the hundred grand today. Don't worry about it."

"If I don't get $200,000 today, you'll be sorry."

"Spare me the clichés, Danny. What are you going to do, kill me? Really? You look like someone just beat the hell out of you and you're wearing a girl's T-shirt. I think you have bigger problems than me."

"I WILL kill you. I have that capacity."

"Give me a break. You're desperate; and as far as I can tell, you're in debt to the mob. Get out of here, loser. I'll give you what's left in the Trust, but not a penny more."

My blood was boiling through my veins. I wanted to choke this son-of-a-bitch on the spot. I stood up and pointed at him. "I'll kill you."

"Get out of here," he said.

I slammed the door behind me.

CHAPTER 45

⚜

I couldn't go back to the house for fear of getting caught by the Sheriff. I called Mike's house and asked Mrs. Kingston if she would take care of Money for a few days and she politely agreed. She knew where the house key was and I thanked her for agreeing on such short notice.

I started the El Camino and drove west on Poplar, cautiously towards downtown. Just beyond Le Bonheur Children's Hospital I could see the Pyramid and St. Jude Children's Research Hospital. I stayed on Poplar until I reached 2nd street and took a left. I drove past Beale Street, filled with tourists, and found a parking garage.

I wanted to blend into Beale Street to figure out what to do next and where to go for the night.

One of my favorite places was Silky O'Sullivan's. They served ice cold Yuengling on draft at a reasonable price.

I found an empty stool at the bar and waited for the sexy little blond bartender to make her way to me. A live band was playing and the noise level was nearly unbearable. I fiddled with a coaster and when the little blonde came my way I put my index finger in the air. She came closer and leaned in to hear what I wanted. I had to yell my order to her.

She poured a headed Yuengling and sat it in front of me in a frosty mug. I handed her a credit card. She asked me if I wanted to start a tab. I affirmed with a nod and mouthed to her that she gave good head as I pointed to the top of the mug. She shook her head and mouthed a thank you with a half smile.

I watched the soundless TV over the bar. ESPN was on, reminding me of Travertine. I rubbed the hard bloody knot on my head and grimaced in pain. I took a few gulps and felt a tap on my shoulder.

I turned to see that it was my friend from Officer Candidate School, Paul Naylor. I spun around in the stool. "Hey man!" I yelled. "What the fuck are you doing here?"

Paul leaned in and spoke loudly. "I'm on temporary duty at the Naval Station in Millington. Board support."

"No shit! That's awesome."

"Hey, why don't you join us at the table?"

"Okay."

I informed the little blonde that I was moving over to that table, pointing. She cashed me out and I left her a ten dollar tip.

Paul led me through the crowd to a corner table, far enough from the live band that a conversation was possible without shouting. He introduced me to two other Navy officers, who by now were nearly three sheets to the wind.

I entertained them with episodes from the many women I had been with over the past several months. One of the officers asked me what happened to my head. I brushed it off by saying that I hit it on a piece of farm equipment that morning.

Paul pointed to my T-shirt, laughing. "Dude, where'd you get that shirt?"

"It's Jennifer's. I forgot to take it off before I left the house."

"How is she?" Paul asked.

I explained what happened, sobering the mood at the table.

The waitress stopped by to check on us and they all ordered another beer.

"Put this guy's beer on my tab," Paul said, pointing at me.

"That's not necessary," I said.

"I don't want to hear it. My treat tonight, Zombie!"

"Thanks." I replied.

When the fresh beers arrived, they raised their bottles and Paul gave a toast. "Here's to Danny and his family. May they rest in peace, and may our friend be strengthened and blessed."

"Thanks, guys," I said. "Life goes on, right?"

Paul put his hand on my shoulder. "Everything happens for a reason, buddy. It'll be alright."

I stayed for a few more beers and announced that I had to leave.

"Here, Danny," Paul said, "put my cell number in your phone. And don't be a stranger!"

"Got it. Thanks."

I went to the bathroom and then walked to the parking garage. I sat in the El Camino for an hour wondering how I was going to come up with the money.

It was after six o'clock, but I knew Mike Kingston worked late. I drove to his office, and luckily he was still there with a client.

I sat in the lobby reading the Memphis Business Journal from the stack of magazines on the end table. One of the articles talked about a revitalization project happening downtown, in conjunction with cleaning up all the drugs on the streets. I chuckled, remembering Kurt and Rod talking about cleaning up the streets.

Mike's receptionist entered the lobby and announced that he would see me now.

His office was lined with built-in book cases full of law reviews, case law and the entire set of John Grisham's work. Mike and John became friends after facing each other in court on several occasions. All of the books were signed first editions and Mike was quite proud of them.

The furniture was all antiques acquired at local estate auctions, and his desk dominated the center of the room with neatly stacked files and paperwork. A collection of Mimi Dann pottery adorned several places throughout the office.

He told me to take a seat as he sat down in his antiquated squeaky desk chair.

"Did you call the Sheriff?" he asked.

"I have bigger fish to fry."

He looked at my shirt, injured wrists and bloody knot above my ear. "You okay, Danny? You look like you've been through the ringer. Martha said you asked her to watch Money."

"Travertine got ahold of me," I said, rubbing my forehead. I was exhausted.

Mike shook his head in disapproval. "I don't know what to say, Danny. The mob is after you, and you're a suspect in a missing-persons case."

I took a deep breath. "I can handle it."

Mike's secretary interrupted with a knock and opened the office door. "Sorry, Mike. Just wanted to let you know I'm going home. You need anything?"

"No. Thanks. See you tomorrow."

Mike turned his attention back to me. "What you need to do is call the Sheriff. Here," he said, pushing his desk phone toward me, "call him right now."

"Like I said before, this is all a coincidence."

"Then you shouldn't have an issue calling."

"I need to pay the mob first. I'm dead if I don't. I think that's a little more important than calling the Sheriff."

I stood up to walk out.

"Where are you staying tonight?"

"I don't know, but I'll figure it out. Can I use your secretary's computer? I have to look up something."

"Sure."

He escorted me to the computer and returned to his office. I looked up Derrick Geyser's address, put it in Googlemaps, and then printed it out. I stuck my head in Mike's office, "Thanks, Mike. I'll be in touch."

"Be careful, Danny. Call me tomorrow."

"Sure thing."

CHAPTER 46

I drove to the Guns 'N Ammo shop on Summer Avenue. I knew the owner, Jake, who had been an acquaintance of my father for many years. I last saw Jake at the funeral and remembered him telling me that if I ever needed anything to be sure to call.

I walked into the gun shop and asked for Jake. After a few minutes he came out and greeted me with a handshake and man-hug. He was overweight, harry, middle-aged, and wore too much Hai Karate cologne. He smelled like my dad. Those old farts never graduated to Drakkar.

"How you doin', Danny?"

"I'm okay, Jake. Really good to see you."

"What brings you here?"

"I need a small favor."

"Okay."

"I need a 9mm Glock."

"Step back here," he said, escorting me to a small office in the corner, shutting the door. "I'm assuming you can't wait the mandatory federal time. Need it now, right?"

"Yes."

"I'm not going to ask why, Danny. I trust everything is okay. Can't say I'm diggin' your shirt though."

"Don't have time to explain it, but I promise you it's all good. I just need some protection at the farm. Dad's guns are locked in the gun vault and I don't have the combo."

"I can't sell it to you, Danny, but I know a guy that can. Let me make a quick call. Do you mind stepping out for a moment?"

"No problem," I replied.

I browsed the gun shop for a few minutes and then Jake called me back into the office. He handed me an address. "Meet him here in thirty minutes. He'll be driving a black Ford F-150 pickup."

"Thanks, Jake. I owe you."

"No you don't. Just stay out of trouble. If you get caught with it, you don't know me."

"Got it. Do you know how much?"

"$1,000."

"Good enough. Thanks again, Jake."

I pulled the money out of a local ATM. I saw the balance in my account was over $200,000. Derrick had made the wire transfer for $100,000. I felt somewhat relieved, but I still needed another hundred grand.

I drove around for a while, stopped at a mini-mart for a Coke, bought a small cigar and sat in the parking lot and smoked it. Thirty minutes felt like two hours.

I finally drove to the meeting place - an abandoned bowling alley on Summer Avenue. A black Ford truck with shiny chrome wheels, low profile tires and dark-tinted windows was parked near the rear of the building, just beyond a faint plume of an old pole light.

I pulled up and got out. The man rolled down his passenger side window and told me to get in.

The dash lights were dim, but I could see that he was wearing a Memphis Grizzlies hat and a black shirt with a large gold cross hanging low on his chest. He didn't smile, but I could see several gold teeth as he spoke.

He showed me the gun and a box of ammo.

"How much?" I asked.

"Twelve fifty."

"Jake said it would be a grand," I replied.

"Look, man, I ain't got all night."

I dug through my pockets and wallet. "I got another fifty here."

"That'll do, dog, if Jake wants to skip his normal take."

"You pay Jake $200 for referrals?"

"Straight up, dog."

"Look, Jake called you. Why would he say a grand and now you're telling me twelve fifty? You hustlin' me?"

"Give me the goddamn money and get the fuck out. You forget you ever saw me if you get caught."

"Understood."

I sat in the El Camino, loaded the Glock and placed it under my seat.

I called Paul and asked if it was possible to bunk up with him for the night at the Naval Base. He was more than happy to help me out.

I started the El Camino, eased out of the dimly lit parking lot and drove to the Naval Base in Millington. Paul met me at the gate and signed me in.

We were hungry, so we drove to a place in Millington called Old Timers. We ate chicken wings, fries, salad, and guzzled several Yuenglings.

There was an autographed photo of Justin Timberlake on the wall next to our table. Paul asked the waitress about it. She said Justin grew up in Millington and came into the restaurant often when he was home.

"Interesting," Paul said.

I paid the bill, left a large tip, and we went back to Paul's room for a nightcap of Bud Lights.

The last thing I remembered was stammering about how much I missed Jennifer.

CHAPTER 47

❦

I woke up the next morning, Thursday, at 7:00 a.m., showered quickly, and thanked Paul for his hospitality.

On the way to Memphis I pulled out the printed Googlemap of Derrick's address.

Fifty minutes later I was parked in front of Derrick's house in a posh neighborhood in Germantown, hoping to catch him leaving for work. I was listening to the Kurt and Rod morning show. They were discussing a section of the program called *Dumb Asses Of The Day* – true stories about stupid criminals. Kurt talked about a man who walked into a convenience store to steal a case of beer. As he was sneaking out, the cashier yelled, "I need to see your identification even if you aren't going to pay for that!" They guy showed her his driver license. The cops showed up at his door a half hour later and arrested him.

Rod started to read the next story as something caught my eye. Derrick came out the front door and was walking to his car. I started the El Camino and blocked the end of the driveway. I grabbed the Glock from under the seat and jumped out.

Derrick saw me approaching with the gun. He dropped his briefcase and raised his hands. "Take it easy, Danny. What the fuck are you doing?"

"I told you I'd kill you."

"I transferred the hundred grand."

"I told you to transfer two hundred."

"I don't have it. I don't. Honestly."

I stopped three feet from him and pointed the barrel at his head. "Get it. Get it today. Or I'm going to carve a valley through your fucking skull."

"I'll get it, Danny. Just give me time. Please, put that gun down."

"Time is not something I have. You need to get it today."

"Okay. Okay," he said, begging. "Please, put that thing away. I'll get it today."

I stepped closer. "Do you love your wife and kids?"

"Leave them out of this. I promise you, I'll get the money today."

"I need cash."

"I can do that."

"I'll stop by your office this afternoon and you'd better have the cash. A hundred grand. No less."

I backed away, got into the El Camino and squealed away.

I needed somewhere to hole up until the afternoon.

My cell phone rang. I turned off the radio.

"Hello."

"Be at the JC Penny parking lot at the Wolfchase Mall at 9:00."

"Why?"

The caller hung up. I didn't recognize the voice, but I knew it had to be Travertine.

I drove to the closest First Tennessee Bank. It was 8:30. I was thankful the lobby had just opened.

I filled out a withdrawal slip for $200,000 and handed it to the teller.

"May I see some I.D. sir?" she asked.

I handed her my license.

"Thank you, Mr. Dedd. Whom would you like the cashier's check made payable to?"

"I don't want a check. I need it all in cash. $100 bills, please."

"Oh. One moment, sir."

She wasn't an attractive girl, but she had nice skin. She exited the teller area and went into the branch manager's office. She returned to her station a few minutes later. "Uh, it's going to be a few minutes, Mr. Dedd. We have to get the cash out of the vault. Would you please have a seat?"

"I don't have much time. Could you please hurry?"

"Yes, sir."

I took a seat in the lobby and could see the branch manager and teller entering the vault behind the teller line.

I noticed my leg twitching up and down on the ball of my foot.

The lobby had a lavender odor. A large black woman walked past me in a cloud of patchouli. I hated patchouli. I held off a gag.

The branch manager approached me. "Mr. Dedd, please come with me." I caught her looking at my shirt and grinning.

She escorted me to a private room beside the vault, where the teller was standing beside stacks of hundreds on a small table in the middle of the room.

"Mr. Dedd, we are going to count this in front of you and I will need you to sign this document acknowledging that you received $200,000 cash."

"Sure. Please make it quick."

"Yes, sir."

"Can you tell me the time?" I asked.

"It's 8:45."

"Thank you."

"My pleasure."

The teller began to count it aloud. I leaned against the wall. My leg started to quiver again. I took a deep breath.

The teller was counting slower than a sloth. "Forty eight thousand, forty nine thousand, fifty…"

"Can you tell me the time again, please?"

"8:55."

"Is she almost done?" I asked.

The branch manager held up her finger as if to say "Shhh." I saw her lips moving with the teller's counting.

"$200,000. It's all there," declared the teller.

"Okay, Mr. Dedd," asked the manager, "would you like to count it, too?"

"No. Just put it in a bag. I'm late."

The teller pulled out a cloth bag from under the table and put all the stacks into it.

"Please sign here, Mr. Dedd. Would you like security to walk you to your car?"

"No," I said.

I signed the paper and dashed to the El Camino.

CHAPTER 48

I pulled into the JC Penny parking lot fifteen minutes late. *I'm fucking dead*, I thought. I found an empty section at the far end of the lot. The *Lone Eagle Bakery* van pulled in beside me

The burly man got out and walked around to my door. I sat there with my window down, not making eye contact, waiting for a punch or gun to my head.

"Hey, Danny, bet you're glad to see me again, eh?"

"Delighted."

He instructed me to get into the van with him. When I got into the passenger side someone behind me grabbed my arm and said to come to the back of the van. I was forced onto the floor, where I was blindfolded, gagged and handcuffed.

I estimated the van drove for about fifteen minutes. I heard a garage door closing and the back door of the van opened. I was pulled out and escorted to a musty room. They sat me in a stiff chair. I surmised that I was back in the torture room. The odor was the same.

They removed my blindfold and gag. Franco was there, sitting in a chair in front of me again.

"Can you remove the handcuffs too?" I asked.

"No," Franco said, "you got the money?"

"Yes. All two hundred grand."

"Very good. Where is it?"

"In my car."

The burly man entered the room carrying the cloth bag. "Here it is, boss."

"Count it," said Franco.

The burly man started to dump it onto the floor.

"No, you stupid ass! Take it out there and the three of you count it!"

"Oh. Okay, boss."

I chuckled, looking at Franco. "Does he know how to count?"

"I'm not sure," said Franco. "Nice shirt, by the way."

"Thanks," I said. "It was on sale at CVS."

Franco snickered. "I like you, Danny. It's unfortunate that we find ourselves in this situation. I can imagine us in another life plowing the froth off a couple beers with some three-cheese penne."

"Yeah. That would be cool."

"Nonetheless, you did good today. $200,000. What about the other hundred grand?"

"You agreed to $200,000 today and the rest tomorrow."

"Yes, I did."

"What if I can't come up with the hundred grand tomorrow?"

"I think you know the answer to that, Danny."

"I've got a Lear Jet worth well over a million."

"And what am I going to do with a fucking jet?"

"I don't know. Fly it?"

Franco laughed. "What else you got?"

"A farm. Over a thousand acres."

"Well, now, that peeks my interest. Is it clear?"

"What do you mean?"

"Do you owe any money on it?"

"No."

"I'll make arrangements to get it signed over. In the meantime, don't leave town. If you do, the deal is off and the hundred grand triples, and I also get the farm. Am I clear?"

"Crystal."

Franco poured some liquid on a cloth and said "Nighty night."

CHAPTER 49

I woke up in the El Camino. I watched people come and go from the mall. I saw families, couples, old people and children, all seemingly happy. I remembered being happy once.

I heard a beautiful voice coming from nowhere. *"Come back to me, Danny. I need you. Little Danny needs you. Come, be with us."*

I looked around. Nobody was within fifty feet of the El Camino. I shook my head and took a deep breath. *I must be crazy.*

I started the El Camino and backed out of the parking spot. *I'm not losing that farm*, I thought. *It's time to come clean.*

I called Mike and asked if we could call the Sheriff together. He told me to come right over.

I hit a McDonalds drive-thru and ate lunch on the way.

Mike's secretary showed me right in.

"Good to see you, Danny," Mike said.

"You too, Mike."

"Ready?"

"Yep."

He put the phone on speaker and dialed the number. A lady transferred the call to the Sheriff. Mike explained that he had me in his office and we would be happy to answer any questions.

The Sheriff explained that the Las Vegas police called because they were investigating several cases of missing girls, and the investigators discovered that each time one of the girls went missing Danny's airplane was logged into the airport.

"Danny," said the Sheriff, "I need to ask you a few questions."

"Okay."

"How many times have you flown to Las Vegas over the past twelve months?"

"Probably five times, but I'd have to check my log book."

"Could it have been thirteen?"

"Possibly."

"Did you bring anyone back with you from Las Vegas?"

"Yes."

"Who?"

"Derrick Geyser."

"Who's that?"

"A financial advisor. He was my guest. He lives and works here in Memphis."

"Did you bring any girls home with you?"

"Nope."

"Interesting. Three of the missing girls called their friends and said they were in Mississippi with a guy named Danny. So let me ask you again. Did you bring any girls home with you?"

Mike stopped me as I started to answer. "Don't answer that. It's hearsay."

"Danny," said the Sheriff, "there's enough circumstantial evidence to get a search warrant for the farm."

Mike interrupted. "Danny is not answering any more questions, Sheriff. I'm going to end this call now." He pushed the speaker button to disconnect the call.

Mike looked at me like he never had before. "What the hell have you gotten yourself into, son?"

"This is all coincidence, Mike. I didn't kidnap anyone."

"Nobody said anything about kidnapping. I'll try to stall the search warrant for as long as I can. In the meantime, you need to go home and stay there. Oh, and did you work things out with Travertine?"

Without hesitation I blurted out, "Yes." I resisted the urge to ask Mike for a hundred grand, not wanting him to be involved in this mess.

"Good. Go home."

"I will….hey Mike."

"Yeah?"

"I've never said this to you before, but I love you like a father. I just want you to know that."

Mike paused. "I love you too, Danny. Now go home."

CHAPTER 50

I called Derrick on my way back to the homestead.

"I told you I'd get the hundred grand today," Derrick said.

"Don't worry about the hundred grand."

"What?" Derrick asked.

"You heard me right."

"This morning you wanted to kill me."

"I just received a phone call from Mike. A wealthy Memphis family wants to buy the farm for three million dollars."

"Interesting."

"I'm sorry for threatening your family, Derrick. It was a desperate moment. You know I wouldn't have hurt them."

"I know. You don't have an evil bone in your body. You wouldn't hurt a flea if it was biting Money."

I was amused that he was so forgiving, yet it's what I hoped for. "Let me make it up to you, Derrick. Are you busy later?"

"Maybe."

"Do you want to go to Vegas?"

"Not sure. This is all weird."

"It's all good. Seriously. I feel so bad about what I've done. I'd like to treat you to Vegas. Just you and me."

"Only if you pay for everything, Danny, and you have me back here by tomorrow evening."

"Done. Be at the farm tonight at 9:00, sharp. The Jennifer is taking off, with our without you."

"Don't worry, I'll be there."

What an idiot, I thought.

I called Mike. "Were you able to delay the search?"

"The Sheriff agreed to hold off for twenty four hours, that's all. He owed me a favor. I got him out of a DUI a few years back. Saved his job."

"Thanks, Mike. I need another favor."

"What's that?"

"Can you and Martha keep Money for a while?"

"Why?"

"I just need some time alone. When I'm there he is constantly wanting attention. I can't get a good night's sleep."

"You know we'll watch him. I'm just concerned that you are up to something."

"No worries, Mike. You know what I've been through. I just need some down time."

"Don't do anything stupid, Danny."

"I'm okay. Really."

"I hope so. I'll be there tomorrow when the Sheriff arrives."

"Thanks, Mike."

CHAPTER 51

I arrived at the homestead. Luckily there were a few Yuenglings left in the fridge. I took a shower, changed into clean jeans and an AC/DC T-shirt, ate a sandwich, drank the Yuenglings, and then sat on the front porch for a moment.

I went inside, and then returned to the porch with two tall lamps. I sat them on either side of the door, plugged them in, removed their shades and turned them on. I turned on the porch lights. I went back inside and grabbed a surgical mask and walked out to the Quonset hut to visit the girls.

I walked in with the mask over my mouth and sat Indian style in front of the stacks of bodies. I addressed each one by name and told them how much fun I had with them, and apologized for taking them out of this world so soon.

I told them life was short anyway, and that I would see them on the other side soon, and not to be mad at me; and if they knew Jennifer they would know why I did what I did.

I hoped that they had met her already in Heaven and were having a great time talking about all the good times they had with me.

I walked to the big barn to check on The Jennifer. I ran my hands all around her and gently rubbed the engines. I walked to the front and kissed her nose and told her that I loved her. I apologized for what I was about to do.

I heard Derrick pull up the driveway, so I went outside to motion him into the barn. I loaded his bag, opened the barn doors, and fired up the engines.

Derrick was oblivious to the fact that I didn't bother going through the checklist. He was in the co-pilot seat and said he couldn't wait to get to the poker table.

I looked at him and smiled.

I taxied The Jennifer onto the runway and immediately went full throttle up.

Derrick clenched the arm rests. "I never get tired of this, Danny. Wow!"

I turned a sharp left to circle toward the house. "Hold on, Derrick. I'm gonna kick her in the ass!"

I aligned The Jennifer square on the house and took her into a steep nose dive, gaining speed as she angled toward the lit-up porch.

"What are you doing?" Derrick yelled.

"No worries, asshole, it's just a fly-by!"

"Oh my god!"

The explosion was heard several miles across the delta as flames lit up the sky.

CHAPTER 52

⁙

I was floating within a massive black expanse, yet everything was visible. My consciousness expanded beyond the edge of the universe and I could see 360 degrees. There was no sense of self, just oneness with everything and everyone. *This must be what the Buddhists call Nirvana, or maybe this is Heaven.*

I understood that I was absolute energy with and without structure, hovering in nothingness, divinely organized as a part of the whole. I was consumed with a peace that passed all understanding. Time and matter were of no importance, and all the love of the universe was present, encompassing, and overwhelming.

I perceived a spec of light a million light years away. I went to it instantly just by observing it. It grew as I approached. A perfect circle of light with a hazy rim, purity spilling from its edges, growing from a blurry dot into majestic clarity. I found myself inside of it.

There were humanlike figures of pure light standing in its midst, staring at me, offering me all their love. There were other shadowy figures who slowly formed into shapes of humans.

I reached out to one of them. I wanted to shout her name but I couldn't speak. Her love engulfed me, comforted me, and I heard her tell me everything was okay, that she and little Danny were waiting for me.

As soon as she said this I was pulled away, back into the expanse, away from the circle of light.

I reached out for her as I floated farther and farther away. The circle dissipated into nothingness.

CHAPTER 53

⸎

I was taken to the homestead, watching the flames shoot into the evening sky as an army of firemen from Tunica County did their best to douse them. Blue and red flashing lights filled the area. Onlookers lined Highway 61. Reporters from Memphis were begging authorities to let them get closer. Cameras in helicopters were capturing it all.

I realized that I could now reposition myself just by thinking about it. I wanted to get closer to the guest house and I was instantly there. And I was able to hear people's thoughts and intentions.

The Sheriff was talking to Mike. I placed myself beside them. Mike told the Sheriff there was no use trying to delay the search warrant and to go ahead with his search when it was safe to do so. The Sheriff said he had a hunch that he would find something bad there. Mike told him he hoped his hunch was wrong.

Mike was thinking how disappointed he was in me and was asking himself how I could do such a thing as kidnap girls and destroy my family's home.

The Sheriff was thinking that he would get this son-of-a-bitch and it served this family right to all die, as they refused to support local law enforcement charities. He justified in his mind that this was a fitting end to rich fucking snobs.

I felt no ill will toward the Sheriff. I could only send love and kindness to him.

The Sheriff called a crew of his deputies into a huddle and told them to search every building on the premises with a fine toothed comb. I wanted them to find it all.

The Sheriff walked to the small barn. There was a pad lock on it, so he asked one of the firemen to bring him a pair of bolt cutters. The deputies that were searching the guest house found nothing of interest, so they all made their way to the small barn where the Sheriff was removing the lock. I heard their thoughts as they waited for the doors to open.

One of the firemen was a Navy veteran and served on the USS Enterprise with me, although I didn't know him then. He remembered seeing me come and go from sortie runs, although he knew I would never remember such a peon as he.

When I heard this man's thoughts I went back to the ship. I was walking off the flight deck and someone handed me a bottle of water as I exited my F-14D Tomcat. It was this fireman. I remembered that I never thanked him for it. I reached out to hug him, but my arms swished through his body.

The Sheriff removed the lock and two deputies helped him open the doors. The first thing they saw was Sarah's pink VW Beetle. I heard the Sheriff think, *we got you, you bastard.*

He directed one of his deputies to run the Nevada license plate. The keys were in the ignition. He started the Beetle and backed it out of the barn.

I remember the last time I rode in that Beetle, from McCarran International Airport to the German restaurant, and then to Sarah's apartment. I felt an endearing love for Sarah and wished she was there so I could apologize for what I had done to her.

Beyond the Beetle were all of Sarah's belongings from her apartment. The deputies sifted through them, commenting on how many pink things there were…pink lamps, pink blankets, pink shoes, pink clothes, pink everything. I chuckled, *she sure loved pink*.

The Sheriff's scavenger hunt was interrupted by an excited deputy who had information from the tags he ran through the database. He handed a piece of paper to the Sheriff who read it aloud. "Sarah Walthall, 113 Brevard Avenue, Apartment 603, Las Vegas, Nevada." The Sheriff pulled out his notepad and flipped through the pages. His thoughts were self-glorifying, and then he announced to everyone that Sarah was one of the girls that was reported missing from Las Vegas when Danny Dedd's airplane was logged at the airport, and that they needed to search the remainder of the buildings on the premises.

Deputies scurried like ants whose hill had just been disturbed by the shoe of a curious little boy.

I hovered over the Quonset hut, waiting for the deputies to make their way there. They found nothing of interest in all the other buildings. The Sheriff pointed at the hut and told them to search it.

CHAPTER 54

꩜

I was floating again in the black expanse. I went to the circle of light.

The beings were there. They told me how much they loved me, and I could feel Jennifer stroking my hair and face. My father was holding little Danny, who looked like a perfect mix of Jennifer and me. I felt a love toward this little being unlike any other in the universe.

I wanted resolution to this dream or whatever it was, and I was not buying into what was being presented. Was this the torture of Hell, where I would spend eternity seeing my loved ones but never able to converse with them or feel their bodies? I'd rather be writhing in eternal flames, gnashing my teeth where the worm dies not.

I caught my son's thought. He wanted his daddy to hug and play with him. *Torture*, I thought, *all torture, goddamn it!*

CHAPTER 55

❦

I was transported back to the Quonset hut where the Sheriff and his deputies continued their search.

The Sheriff opened the door and was wracked with an overwhelming odor of decaying flesh. He fell to the ground, coughing. Mike was there and I heard him think, *oh my god, Danny, what have you done?*

The Sheriff gathered himself and told the deputies to get gas masks. Impatience drove him to pull up his T-shirt collar from under his uniform and stretch it over his nose. He walked into the hut, but his shirt was not enough to quell the smell, so he retreated in disgust.

The deputies found a few masks in the trunks of their patrol cars and borrowed a few from the firemen and came running to the hut. I heard one of the firemen ask what was going on. A deputy said he didn't know but it must be bad if the boss wanted gas masks.

The raging fire from the house was nearly extinguished and no longer provided light for the search. The deputies arrived at the Quonset hut with gas masks, but it was too dark to see anything inside. The Sheriff ordered search lights to be brought to the area.

Mike was standing beside the Sheriff thinking of a way to stop the search. I heard him thinking of how he needed to be loyal to the Dedd family, no matter the cost. Mike told the Sheriff that there was no need to go into the hut because what he smelled was rotting deer carcasses that I had killed a couple weeks ago. The Sheriff informed Mike that he already had enough evidence to prove Danny kidnapped at least one of the girls, and he owed it to the other girls' families to get the truth.

Three firemen and two deputies arrived with flood lights. They ran extension cords from the guest house to the Quonset hut. The flood lights were placed in front of the door to light up the inside.

The Sheriff put on a gas mask and went inside. His leg caught the wheel barrel handle, causing him to stumble. I heard some of the bystanders laugh in their minds.

The Sheriff composed himself and walked to the first stack of bodies, kneeling in front of them. He thrust his hand into the pile of dirt and pulled on something. An arm slowly revealed itself. The Sheriff announced that this was a dead human body and directed someone to call the coroner.

I was instantly transported to the crowd of bystanders on Highway 61. Mrs. Kingston was there holding Money with loving adoration, stoking him as he nuzzled himself against her bosom.

I heard Money's thoughts…he wanted to sit beside the kitchen table and eat treats, rub against my legs and sleep beside me on the sofa. I reached out for him. He hissed and showed his teeth. Mrs. Kingston consoled him and told him everything would be alright.

I was taken back to the Quonset hut, where everyone was waiting for the coroner to arrive. One of the firemen said they were able to enter the house and found the charred remains of humans.

They found three mangled legs and two scorched heads. Mike and the Sheriff rushed over to the house to view the remains.

Mike was able to identify me. I looked at my head and was filled with sadness. I felt sorry for that person. He lost his way. I wished I could talk to him now. I'd tell him everything would be okay. He didn't have to replace Jennifer. She was in a wonderful place. Just go on with life and be happy.

Mike said the other head looked familiar and might be Derrick Geyser. I stared at Derrick's charred face, surprised that all I felt was love for his lost soul.

The coroner arrived on the scene and asked that everyone stand clear of the area. She and her team of crime scene investigators scoured the Quonset hut for evidence. They took flesh samples from each body and from Derrick's and my remains.

CHAPTER 56

I floated away from the homestead. I tried to fight the force that was taking me, but I had no control over it. I rose up into the night sky as the Earth ran away from view.

I felt a sharp pain in my arm as I came to a halt inside the endless black expanse. Someone kissed me on the cheek and stroked my hair.

I saw something materialize in front me, like a large movie screen. I watched it replay my life from infancy.

I saw my birth. The love emanating from my mother was overwhelming.

My father held me in the nursery and told me how much he loved me. I wondered when my father stopped telling me that; I could not remember him ever saying it, except for the day I returned home from basic training.

I saw my mom holding me in bed, breast feeding.

My father was changing my diaper and I peed on his face. I saw my parents laughing.

I was sitting on my new Huffy motocross bicycle. My father had just removed the training wheels and was holding me upright. He gave me a gentle push down the driveway, and I took off yelling and screaming with joy. A tear rolled down my father's cheek.

It was Christmas and I was six years old when I got my first model airplane kit. I saw myself opening it, a World War II era B-52 bomber. The feeling of fresh discovery came rushing back. My father helped me build it and hang it over my bed.

At ten years old my father made arrangements for us to take a ride in a small Cessna airplane. We dipped past the house, and then flew along the Mississippi River to Memphis. The man let me steer the plane for a few minutes, instructing me to follow the river. The buildings downtown looked small. It was the moment I knew I wanted to be a pilot.

I watched myself graduate from high school on a sunny afternoon. When I got home my father told me to go to the barn to get a tool. I opened the barn door and there it sat, my 1959 El Camino, midnight blue Speedline Bel-Air body, chrome wheels and trim, with a full-size grill for optimal air intake to the 348 Turbo Thrust V8 engine. I knew it by heart because it's all I talked about for the previous two years in high school. My parents stood on the porch, holding each other, happy. My father yelled and said the keys were in it if I wanted to take it for a ride.

I drove slowly down the driveway, stopped on Highway 61, and then revved it up and burned rubber down the road. My mom put her hand over her mouth as my father yelled "That's my boy!"

I was now sitting in History class, freshman year at Ole Miss. Jennifer was walking to class with wet hair, wearing pink shorts and a white blouse.

The movie stopped.

I began to move once more against my will.

CHAPTER 57

I was hovering over Derrick Geyser's front yard as a Memphis police car pulled into the driveway. The officer stepped out and walked to the front door and knocked. Mrs. Geyser answered with a puzzled look on her face. The policeman explained that he regretted to tell her that her husband was killed in an airplane crash in Tunica County.

She put both hands over her mouth and said she knew this would happen. She told the policeman that Derrick was never home and hoped that someday the unfaithful bastard would end up dead somewhere. She was looking forward to collecting his life insurance.

Suddenly I was in a room with two men, whom I recognized as Franco and the burly man. They were counting money on a table and smoking cigarettes. Another man came in and asked if they heard the news - Danny Dedd flew his plane into his house and killed himself and Derrick Geyser. Franco slapped the table and called me a crazy mother fucker. He was angry about Derrick dying because he still owed $50,000.

I laughed.

CHAPTER 58

I was back in the black expanse, floating again toward the light. There were more than four shapes within it now. My father was holding little Danny. Mike Kingston and his wife were there, which seemed very odd to me.

I felt my spirit take on flesh, and a rush of pain dominated my body as everything faded to black.

I felt a bed beneath me and heard machines beeping and swishing.

Through the pain I struggled to open my eyes, and I heard Jennifer shout, "He moved his eyes! He moved his eyes!"

My vision was blurry as I blinked frantically to bring everything into focus. I tried to speak but a tube down my throat prevented it. Both of my legs were in casts and my mom was rubbing my cold toes and crying profusely.

Needles were stuck in both arms, and there was a burning sensation in my penis.

I felt someone squeeze my hand. I tried hard to focus. It was Jennifer! Her tears dropped onto my cheek as she kissed me over and over.

I heard my father ask Mike to please run and get the doctor.

I looked at Jennifer. She was more beautiful now than I could ever remember.

My father brought little Danny closer so he could touch my arm. I was able to lift my hand and squeeze little Danny's fingers. They were long and soft, much like mine. He had an angelic glow and the most precious thing I'd ever seen. He had Jennifer's tan hue and dark eyes, with my nose and mouth.

My father smiled like he was holding a prized trophy. My mom kissed me on the forehead and told me how much she loved me and how glad they were to have me back.

Mrs. Kingston said, "Welcome back, Danny. We missed you!"

Mike came back into the room with the doctor. He inspected my eyes with a bright pen light. "He's back," he said. "Remarkable."

I recognized the doctor. He was an unusually large man who would probably have to buy two airline tickets because he couldn't fit into one seat. I managed a smile that apparently nobody saw. His nametag read *Dr. Chuck Timblin.*

I heard them discussing whether my mental capacity would be what it once was, and Dr. Chuck explained that only time would tell. I wanted to shout that I was okay, but instead I could only raise my hand and give a thumbs-up.

Dr. Chuck said they would run some tests the next day to determine my mental condition and would monitor my physical progress closely. He cautioned them that under the best of circumstances, it would still be a long road to recovery.

CHAPTER 59

On the third day after opening my eyes, the feeding and breathing tubes were removed. Dr. Chuck told me to ease into speaking because I could damage my vocal chords if I pushed it too hard. I was hungry, and I mused at the thought of asking him to fix me a sandwich, but I didn't want to be rude.

Everyone was astounded at how quickly I was recovering after being in a coma for so many months.

Jennifer was at my side the whole time, sleeping in my room on a cot. My parents were more than happy to watch little Danny during this time. Robert and Judy drove in from Huntsville several times to help out.

When my voice came back, I asked Jennifer what happened.

"What's the last thing you remember, baby?" she asked.

"Well, I remember you being pregnant. You moved back to the guest house. I came back from Pensacola and you all died in a car accident. My life took a terrible turn at that point. Then I flew my plane into the house, killing me and Derrick Geyser. And then I woke up here."

"Well," Jennifer said, "the part about me moving back to the guest house is accurate. But here we are, baby, we're not dead."

"What happened?"

"You were in an accident. Your plane went down off the coast of Pensacola. They said you lost power over a residential area, but you miraculously stayed with it until you were over water and then ditched into the gulf. They said you didn't eject until a few feet from hitting the water. You were unconscious when the Coast Guard pulled you out. You've been in a coma for several months, sweetheart."

"That's crazy. I don't remember any accident."

I pulled Jennifer into my arms, grateful that I was again holding the love of my life.

Someone knocked and asked if it was okay to come in.

"How ya doin' Danny?"

I furled my eyebrows. "Derrick?"

"Hey, you remember me!"

He shook my hand as Jennifer excused herself to get me a cup of hot tea and a snack.

The TV was on ESPN, prompting Derrick to break into a sports conversation.

"You miss watching all the games, Danny? Ole Miss had a great season."

I snickered. "Actually, I'm partial to horse racing."

"Well," Derrick replied, "I know a good bookie if you need one."

"His name wouldn't happen to be Joseph, would it?"

"Yeah. How'd you know?"

EPILOGUE

I remember the first time I saw Jennifer at Ole Miss. It was our first semester, sophomore year, 2007. We were in World History class in Conner Hall, one of the original buildings on campus, containing four large classrooms with auditorium-style seating.

I sat in the middle of the second row so I could hear the professor clearly. My dad advised me that most professors formulate their tests from their lectures, so be sure to sit close and pay attention.

I majored in Criminology. My plans were to join the Navy after graduation to become a Naval Aviator.

Jennifer was a Business major. She was a high-school valedictorian from Huntsville High School, Huntsville, Alabama.

On the first day of class, Jennifer stepped into the middle of the second row near me. "Excuse me," she said, "is this seat taken?"

I looked up from where this angelic voice emanated. Unable to articulate a complete sentence, "Uhhh ... no," I mumbled.

"Mind if I sit beside you?"

"Yes ... I mean, no! Please do!"

She wore pink polyester shorts held up by a narrow white belt, with a white silky blouse. The V cut revealed a bit of cleavage.

Apparently she had just taken a shower. Her damp hair swished against my right cheek as she sat down. She put her book bag on the floor between her legs.

My face was hot, and my heart was pumping a rush of blood southward. *She smells incredible*, I thought.

I placed my hand on my knee closest to her. At an opportune moment I nudged my leg towards her, causing the back of my hand to momentarily touch her naked upper thigh. "I'm sorry," I said.

"It's okay," she replied, blushing.

The professor started the lecture. Jennifer reached down to retrieve a notebook from her book bag, and I leaned forward in hopes of a lucky glimpse at her perky, pristine breasts, resting peacefully in her sports bra. *Wow*, I thought, *amazing*.

She sat up with her notebook, noticing my attention.

"What?" she inquired quietly.

"Oh, nothing," I replied, quickly snapping my head toward the podium.

Our relationship grew at Ole Miss during the first couple months in World History class.

We both felt the pull of more than friendship, but never mentioned it.

One day as we walked out of Conner Hall, I asked her for an evening of study and snacks at the Student Union.

"Study...AND snacks?" she said. "My, you're a big spender, aren't you?"

"Well," I replied, "nothing but the best for my girl." I wasn't sure why I said that. A weak moment, perhaps, or a proclivity to do things on impulse, like the time I punched another boy in seventh grade for cutting in front of me in line. I was suddenly feeling an overwhelming sense of awkward vulnerability.

"YOUR girl?" she asked.

I hesitated, hoping I hadn't pushed her away. "Uhhh....well....I just thought..."

"Thought what?"

"Well, I thought maybe you felt the same way."

"There's a chance I might, but we haven't even been on a date yet."

I felt a hint of relief. "You 'might'?"

"Yes, I might."

"I'll take 'might'."

"Well, 'might' is all you're getting right now, sir."

I offered my arm and smiled. "So, ma'am, would you do me the honor of a first date at the Student Union for study and snacks?"

She took my arm. "Of course, sir, all you had to do was ask. You're such a knucklehead."

"How about 6:00?"

"No."

"No?"

"Yes, 'no', I have to study for a Cost Accounting test. How about 7:00? I'll meet you there."

"Done."

7:00 could not have come soon enough. I was on kitchen duty at the frat house. I helped cook dinner and washed the dishes. A few of the brothers asked me to go to a party off campus.

"No, thanks, I have a date."

"A date?" One of the brothers asked. "Who's the unfortunate lady?"

I flipped him the bird. "Someone worth skipping a party for."

"Dude! Really?" shouted another brother. "Bros before Ho's, man. Bros before Ho's."

"Well," I replied, "She ain't no Ho. She might be THE ONE."

"Oh my god, Danny, don't tell me you're pussy whipped."

That pissed me off, like the kid who cut line in front of me, but I held my composure. "Wait 'til you meet her, man. She's not only hot, she's got a huge brain."

One of the brothers fist-bumped me. "By all means then, you better take care of business, brother."

I arrived at the Student Union at 6:00 to pick out the perfect spot. I chose a booth along the windows overlooking The Grove: a tree-lined, unspoiled, perfectly manicured grassy quad, reserved for wine-toting Ole Miss football fans who gathered there on Saturday mornings before home games – some were spoiled elites who thought they were better than everyone else; but most were genuine, humble human beings who understood that their fortunate place in life was a gift from God and family. I fit in with the latter.

From this booth I would be able to see Jennifer arriving.

I set my watch alarm for 6:45 and dove into my history book. Boring. The chapter was about the English Civil War from 1642 to 1651, a conflict between supporters of King Charles and the Rump Parliament, whatever the hell that was. "Rump Parliament. Really?" I chuckled.

After fifteen minutes on the Battle of Worcester, I folded my arms on the book to rest my head.

I drifted away. My forehead sank through my arms and into the open pages.

"Hey!" Jennifer shouted, poking me on the shoulder. "Sleeping on the first date? How rude!"

I jerked and sat up in a daze. I wiped the string of slobber that stretched from my lower lip to the picture of King Charles. I felt a hot spot on my forehead. The cloudiness of the situation prevented me from speaking right away.

Jennifer laughed, "Ewwwww! Were you dreaming, slobber boy?"

"I guess so," I replied, confused. "Fucking watch. I set the alarm."

"For what time?" Jennifer asked.

"6:45."

"It's 7:30, knucklehead."

"Really?"

"No. I'm just messing with you. It's actually 6:40. I didn't want to be late for our first date. Apparently, you didn't either."

I attempted to wake myself from the daze, shaking my head like a dog after a bath, "Sorry about that."

Jennifer nudged me with her forearm. "Scoot over!"

I was slow to move.

"I mean, if you don't want me to sit beside you…." she said.

I moved toward the window, pulling my book with me. "My bad."

She laid her World History book on the table and plopped down next to me. "That King Charles was a son-of-a-bitch, wasn't he? They beheaded that bastard, and so justified, if I do say so myself."

"What?" I replied, still somewhat groggy.

"I see you didn't get that far in the chapter."

"I guess not."

"So," she said, "where are these snacks you promised me?"

"Right here," I said, reaching for my empty pockets. "Well, I guess I didn't bring any snacks."

She rolled her eyes, "Come on dude; wake up! And you better turn off your watch alarm before it goes off."

"Right. Thanks."

"What's a hungry girl to do? Invited on a snack date with no snacks?"

"Would you like to order some food?"

"Really? What a novel idea. I thought you'd never ask."

"What would you like?"

"I've been known to put a hurting on a cheeseburger and fries."

"And to drink?" I asked.

"Mello Yellow."

"Got it. Cheeseburger, fries, Mellow Yellow. What do you like on your cheeseburger?"

"Tomato, lettuce, pickle and mustard."

"No onion? I love onions on my cheeseburger."

"Well," she replied, "if you eat onions, you seriously diminish your chances of getting your stinky mouth close to mine later."

"No onion! Got it!"

She stood up to let me out of the booth, and gently grabbed my arm. "No onion, dear."

"Right. No onion."

"Are you sure you got it? I mean, you still seem a little groggy, slobber boy."

I furrowed my eyebrows and raised a palm at her. "Don't worry. I got it."

"So sassy!" she said.

I returned with two cheeseburgers, fries and Mellow Yellows. "Here's your cheeseburger, with EXTRA onions!"

"What? You're kidding, right?"

I laughed, "Don't worry. No onions."

I watched her attack the cheeseburger. Another girl doing that would turn me off. But strangely, her doing it was sexy. "You really like that, huh?"

"My favorite meal of all time."

"Interesting. I pegged you as a sophisticated girl who would envy some Beluga caviar with Thornback & Peel crackers."

"Thornback & Peel? Those suck! I'm more of a Jo Malone girl."

I was afraid to ask. "Who is Jo Malone?"

"If I have to explain it to you then you don't deserve to know."

"Sassy," I retorted, picking up my cheeseburger. "Wish I'd have gotten onions now."

She laughed. "Oh, please."

I left half of my fries on the plate. "I'm full."

"You mind if I eat the rest of your fries?"

"Are you serious?"

"Do I look like I'm kidding?"

"No. But how do you keep such a hot figure eating all this food?"

She chuckled through a mouth full of fries. "I've got a great metabolism, I guess."

Dessert was two scoops of my favorite ice cream - Hershey's Chocolate Peanut Butter.

"I thought you were full," she said.

"I'm never too full for Hershey's ice cream. And remember, we have two stomachs – one for the meal and one for dessert."

She laughed and offered to feed me a bite from her spoon.

"Sure," I said.

She scooped a big helping. "Open wide, big boy."

I closed my eyes, enjoying the heap of creamy goodness.

We took turns feeding each other.

When we reached the bottom of the bowl, neither of us wanted the last bite, wanting the other to have it. I scooped up the last puddle of partially melted ice cream and moved it towards her mouth. She refused to open up, so I dotted the end of her nose and then quickly ate the bite. She laughed, wiped it off her nose and rubbed it on my cheek.

"Lick it off," I said.

"Ewww, gross!" she said through laughter.

I explained that to waste a single drop of Hershey's Chocolate Peanut Butter ice cream was a mortal sin. I scraped the ice cream off my cheek and ate it.

"You're a nut," she said.

"Do you mind if I walk you back to your room?" I asked.

"Yes, I do mind," she said, smiling.

I frowned.

"We haven't studied yet. You asked me for a study snack, didn't you?"

"Yes." I reached for my book.

"Yeah. Right, Bobo." She stood up, book in hand. "Let's go."

"Bobo?" I said.

"Yes, 'Bobo'."

"What the hell does 'Bobo' mean?"

"It's my word for silly people. It's nicer than 'Bozo' or 'Dumbass'."

"If you say so."

"Yes, I do say so. How about we take your book to your room and then take mine to my room, and then go for a walk. Sound good?"

"That's a better plan than mine," I replied.

"What was your plan?"

"Stay here and study."

"We could do that. But that would exclude many enjoyable possibilities."

"I like your plan better," I said.

"I thought you would. Study? Really? You are now my number one Bobo."

"Jesus, thanks!" I replied.

"Jesus ain't got nothin' to do with it."

I laughed, "You crack me up."

We walked outside, stopping in The Grove. I cupped her hand. She looked up at me.

"Do you feel it too?" she asked.

I smiled. "I felt it the day you sat beside me in World History."

She sighed in relief. "I didn't want to say anything. I wasn't sure how you felt, and I've never felt like this. It's magic."

We walked hand-in-hand past the Lyceum and down the hill to the Delta Psi house.

"Do you want to see my room?" I asked.

She slapped my shoulder. "Not on the first date!"

"I didn't mean it like that! I just don't want you standing out here alone."

"Yeah. Right, Bobo. I'll wait for you in the foyer."

"Okay, Bobo."

She pointed at me. "Hey, that's MY word, mister!"

I laughed as I hustled my book to my room and returned to the foyer where Jennifer was admiring the house.

"Gosh," she said, "this place is neat and clean. Not what I expected from a bunch of frat boys."

"We all take turns cleaning twice a week," I replied, pointing to a cleaning schedule hanging on the wall. "I had kitchen duty today. It sucks, but it works."

She nodded in agreement. "Impressive."

I opened the front door, escorting her onto the porch. Two of my fraternity brothers stepped aside, allowing us to pass. Jennifer smiled at them. "Thank you."

"Our pleasure, ma'am," one of them replied.

I heard the other one mumble, "Wow, Danny hit the jackpot."

And if I heard it, I'm sure Jennifer did too.

She blushed. I redirected the conversation. "Wow, look at all the stars tonight. You should see how bright they are at my house in Tunica."

She grabbed my hand. "Yes, I'd love to see that."

"May I carry your book?" I offered.

She smiled. "Thought you'd never ask, big fella."

"Big fella? What about Bobo?"

Her eyes glistened as she handed me her book. "Don't worry, you're still my Bobo too."

"Did you ever think I'd break down and ask you for a study snack?" I asked.

"The minute you touched my leg on the first day of class."

"Hey, that was an accident!"

"Yeah. Right!"

We retraced our steps past the Lyceum to the Student Union and The Grove, heading towards Sorority Row. Along the way I lightly massaged the small of her back. We walked in silence most of the way.

She laid her head on my upper arm. "I hope you don't take this the wrong way, but I've never felt so comfortable not talking to someone."

"Funny," I chuckled, "I was thinking the same thing. I wonder why."

"I don't know," she said, "I guess that means...holy cow, did you see that?"

"Oh, my God!" I said, pointing to the sky.

A shooting star lit up campus.

"Did you wish on it?" she asked.

"Of course."

"What did you wish for?"

"You know I'm not supposed to tell."

"I know," she said, "but you can tell me."

"If I tell you, it won't come true. And if it doesn't come true, that means I can't have you."

She stroked my cheek. "That was my wish too."

"Magic," I replied.

We arrived at the rear entrance of the Zeta Tau Alpha sorority house. Her room was on the first floor corner, next to the back door. I handed her the book and she scurried through the door. I sat outside on the steps. I heard her talking to someone in the hallway. They were giggling, and then someone said "You go girl!"

A few minutes passed. She opened the door. I stood up, trying to look behind her. I saw two girls standing in the hallway, pretty, in their nightwear. When they saw me they waved. I waved back. The door shut.

"Who are they?" I asked.

"Oh, just some over-zealous, horny sorority sisters. Let's walk."

I persisted with caution. "They seem nice. What are their names?"

She ignored the question, pulling my hand. "Come on! Don't worry about those girls when you have me right here."

I slapped myself mentally. "Good point."

We strolled back to The Grove and sat on a bench under a large oak tree. She rested her head on my shoulder. I put my cheek against the top of her head.

"Did it hurt?" I asked.

"Did what hurt?"

"When you fell from Heaven."

"Awww. Thank you," she said. "Even though that's one of the oldest pick-up lines in the book, it still makes a girl feel good."

"You ARE an angel, you know."

I kissed the top of her hair. The fragrance caused my blood to rush southward.

I placed her hand on my thigh, stroking the back of it with my thumb. She reached up with her free hand to stroke my short brown hair, and then gently caressed my cheek.

"Your skin is so soft," she said.

"Thanks. I'm big on lotion."

"Me too," she said. "And your hands, they're really big, yet supple. Your fingers are long and soft."

"Gosh," I replied, "nobody has ever referred to my hands as supple. Thanks…I guess."

"Yes, it was a compliment, silly. I have a question for you."

"Okay."

"Who do you look more like, your mother or your father?"

"Great question," I replied. "I get my height and lean build from my father, and I get my blue eyes, dark hair and," making quotes in the air, "'supple' skin from my mother."

She chuckled. "I didn't say you had supple skin. I said you had supple hands!"

I kissed her hand, "Yours are silky smooth, tan and delectable."

She yawned. "Thanks."

"You're either tired or bored. I hope it's the former."

"I guarantee you, I'm not bored. Like I told you before, I have a Cost Accounting test in the morning. I should be going. I need to study for 30 more minutes before bed."

"Only 30 minutes? Sounds like you are ready for it anyway."

"Yes," she replied, "I'd probably get a 98 on the test if I took it now, but I want a hundred."

"Well," I said, "let's stay here a couple more hours and you take that 98!"

"Daniel Dedd! Shame on you, Bobo!"

"Sorry. I tried. I'll escort you back to your room, smarty."

We walked hand-in-hand. She leaned on my arm.

"So," I asked, "what do you want to do after college?"

"Believe it or not, I'm not really sure. I've thought about law school. Ole Miss has a great law program. I've also contemplated a banking career. How about you? What do you want to do?"

"I've always known. I'm going to be a Navy pilot. I want to fly fighter jets. My bedroom at home is filled with model planes hanging from the ceiling that I've built over the years. I feel like I was born to do it."

"That's a gift, Danny. Honor it. No matter what."

"I will."